SUBLIME RECLINE

Other books by Ann LeValley:

April Showers

SUBLIME RECLINE

•

Ann LeValley

AVALON BOOKS
NEW YORK

© Copyright 2004 by Ann LeValley
Library of Congress Catalog Card Number: 2003098880
ISBN 0-8034-9653-2
All rights reserved.
All the characters in this book are fictitious,
and any resemblance to actual persons,
living or dead, is purely coincidental.
Published by Thomas Bouregy & Co., Inc.
160 Madison Avenue, New York, NY 10016

PRINTED IN THE UNITED STATES OF AMERICA
ON ACID-FREE PAPER
BY HADDON CRAFTSMEN, BLOOMSBURG, PENNSYLVANIA

For Chris, Mike, and Heather.

Chapter One

For as long as she could remember, Muffy Sergeant had assumed she would marry James Waite III. So had the fifty guests now standing behind her laughing, drinking, and waiting for James to arrive.

For the last two weeks, she had spent every spare minute organizing this surprise birthday party. With his housekeeper, Glenna Roberts, she had readied the great ballroom of the mansion on his Waitehaven estate. She had persuaded Leah, his excuse for a gardener, to wait in the driveway, distracting him, while she quieted the guests.

Now, she paced behind the front windows, waiting. Outside, the June sun dawdled just above the old Pennsylvania forest, casting long shadows across the vast lawn.

When she'd called the airline, they had told her his flight was on time. He should have missed the rush-hour traffic from Philadelphia. She took a deep breath as the black Mercèdes finally appeared from behind the magnolias.

"HE'S HERE!" she called. "SHHH!"

Laughter stopped. Conversations died. Silk shirts and linen dresses moved toward the door.

The car stopped in front of the wide stone steps. Muffy watched Leah, all dusty, sweaty, and grass-stained, approach it. As James emerged from the car, she saw delight in his eyes.

Just as he reached her, Leah thrust an envelope into his hand, turned, and scrambled into her truck. As she sped off, James opened the envelope, read the note, and grinned.

Muffy's face burned; her heart pounded. *James Waite, are you in love with that stupid gardener? After I've waited years for you to propose to me?*

Muffy stared at the man she'd known all her life, realizing she didn't know him at all. She kept her burning face toward the window and forced her foot not to tap.

The crowd murmured. Muffy turned and put a shushing finger to her lips. She wanted this awful moment over. It was supposed to be an instant of surprise and delight.

Turning back to the window, she watched him pop the trunk open and retrieve his bags. Finally, he plodded up the steps and opened the door.

"SURPRISE! HAPPY BIRTHDAY!" Everyone shouted, laughed, and tried to recapture the gaiety his arrival had squelched.

"Happy thirty-fourth, James." Her forced smile matched his.

"Let me get rid of these bags," he muttered.

She nodded. *And let me get rid of you, James.*

The band used one hurried line of "Happy Birthday" to launch into "My Girl."

Lost in an isolated bubble, she nodded to family friends and childhood friends and Arts Center friends. All that planning for nothing. He was surprised, but neither delighted nor even mildly pleased.

A white-shirted server approached her holding a tray of wine glasses filled with the varieties she had selected. She chose a chardonnay as her best friend, Heather Streker Chandler, appeared with a full smile and a quick hug.

"Was the old bear surprised?" Heather asked.

"What old bear? You mean the one who's gone to his den?" snapped Muffy. "You'd think I'd learn, wouldn't you? Just because I love parties, I always assumed he did."

Sublime Recline 3

When the band paused between songs, she heard the doorbell.

Everyone's here.

Her organizing mind raced through the guest list while the housekeeper bustled to the door. A very tall man with bronze hair, dressed in a tux, entered the room. She had never seen him before.

He carried a big duffle bag and a French easel. At first glance, it looked like a wooden briefcase. As the director of The Arts Center, she'd seen enough students toting their own little wooden boxes to know he was prepared to make pictures.

She saw Mrs. Roberts take his card and scan the crowd. The stranger scanned the crowd too. His gaze stopped at Muffy and his mouth widened into a merry, mischievous smile.

Her breath stopped. For an instant, the room seemed silent. Mrs. Roberts found her too and beckoned.

"Party crasher," Muffy mumbled to Heather. "I shall return."

She marched to the doorway intending to dismiss him, whoever he was, but as she opened her mouth, he said, "You're Muffy. I'll be darned. Wrong dress, but you're gorgeous."

She shrugged the sleeveless shoulders of the plain, cream linen while his whole lean face and green eyes crinkled up in laughter. His hair, unfashionably long and silky clean, had begun to escape from the short ponytail at his neck.

"Who are you?" She hadn't intended to ask with such awe.

"Peter Gant, fine artist. Leah's birthday gift."

"Leah? The garden wrecker?"

"We share an employer. Long story. I'll do charcoal caricatures of anyone and everyone. Out of your way. All I need is a light corner and a couple of chairs."

"Peter Gant? If you were an artist, I'd know you," she said.

His grin broadened. "You will."

Mrs. Roberts patted Muffy's arm. "I'll set him up by the French doors."

As the housekeeper steered him through the crowd toward

the end of the room, he turned back, looked directly at Muffy, and winked. Reluctantly, she smiled back.

"Wrong dress, but you're gorgeous." Has anyone ever called me gorgeous? She glanced down at the offending garment. She hated it too, like all the rest of her clothes.

Looking up, it was easy to watch him traverse the room. He was taller than everyone and all movement stopped as he passed. Muffy started to follow in his wake.

"Muff, how late does this thing last?" James asked.

Her spirits fell with the reappearance of the guest of honor. She compared the somber manner of her companion with the lightness of the stranger.

"Not late. They'll all be gone by ten, maybe eleven if they're having fun." She wanted to tell him to go to bed now before he spoiled the evening for everyone else.

"Have you seen your gift from Leah?" she asked.

"No, but you and I need to talk when everyone leaves."

Good idea, James.

"Fine," she said, "but go meet the artist. He's back there." She nodded toward the knot of guests gathering at the far end of the ballroom.

Collecting kisses on his cheeks and slaps on his back, James vanished.

Muffy returned to Heather, who was lifting a shrimp toast from a server's tray.

"Who's the mystery guest?" her friend asked.

"Some Peter . . . Gant. An artist. A gift from the gardener. Says he's going to do caricatures."

"Well, that's fun. Is he good?"

Muffy shrugged. "I've never heard of him."

"We're looking for a portrait artist, but if you've never heard of him, no one has."

Muffy pictured the four generations of Streker women smiling and trying to pose with three-year-old Becca climbing from one lap to another.

"How's Becca?" asked Muffy.

"We start chemo on Monday."

"Oh, Heather, I'm so sorry. Is there anything I can do?"

"Yes. Find me an artist. One who's patient, fast, and loves squirmy children."

"I'll give you some names tomorrow."

Muffy gave her friend a quick hug as Heather's husband joined them. Turning, she threaded her way through "Great food, Muff," "Excuse me, didn't see you," giant diamond earrings, and the scent of Versace's "Dreamer."

Servers carrying prosciutto-wrapped cantaloupe and tiny skewers of mozzarella and herbs passed more servers carrying trays of zinfandel and chardonnay. On the library table near the stairs, the giant lemon birthday cake sat between stacks of plates and birthday cards.

Just inside the open doors leading to the slate veranda, Peter sat in a Chippendale chair. In a matching chair placed behind the unfolded easel sat an annoyed yet curious James. Muffy followed his eyes to a small aluminum easel displaying an eight-by-ten-inch oil portrait of Leah.

As plain as the woman had always looked to Muffy, this artist had made her look beautiful. He'd tamed her wild hair, blushed her cheeks, and added a glint to her eyes that Muffy had never seen.

She bent closer and noted the edges between the subject and the background. The proportions were perfect and he knew exactly which colors to mix to create lifelike skin tones. She had seen so many amateurs that she immediately recognized professionally trained talent.

Best of all, he had made Leah look pretty without distorting reality. This ability was the essence of every successful portrait artist.

Muffy straightened up and looked at the work in progress. As the artist's hands paused, she burst out laughing. James glowered and Peter turned to her with a grin. "What do you think?" he asked.

"You're a genius," she said.

He glanced between the real James and the snarling charcoal image. After adding a few more dark dashes to the enormous eyebrows, he ripped the paper from the pad and handed it to his subject.

"Do I look that bad?" asked James.

"Worse," said Peter.

The crowd laughed and added their own friendly insults. Peter smiled at Muffy and gestured toward the vacant chair. "Next."

"Me?"

"Especially you."

"Go ahead!," "You're on!," "Do it!" her friends urged.

The chair was still warm from James's body. There had been a time when that would have excited her. Not now.

Yes, James, we will talk when everyone's gone.

"How do you want me?" she asked.

"Bare." Peter laughed out loud. "With your hair down and over your face, just your eyes peeking through. But that's for another time."

Muffy felt her face burn. Unconsciously, she crossed her arms over her chest.

Peter's left hand was already flying over the page.

"Well." She sighed. "Should I smile or anything?"

"Definitely not. Not under the circumstances."

So of course, she did. Couldn't help it.

Peter stopped and studied her face. He leaned closer. "This guy took his pickup to the garage and asked the mechanic how long it would take to inspect it."

Puzzled, Muffy leaned closer to hear him. Her jaw slackened, her lips barely parted, and her eyes focused on Peter's.

" 'An hour,' said the mechanic." Peter was nearly whispering. "When he came back for the truck. . . ."

Muffy leaned closer.

"Right there," commanded Peter. "Hold it. Just like that."

Furiously, he threw the lines on the paper. "Hold it. Hold it," he repeated.

Then he leaned forward, "The mechanic said, 'How could we inspect it when you drove it away?' He'd driven to Kmart to wait!"

Muffy shook her head and answered Peter's smile with her own.

"That's it," he said. "Right there. Don't move."

He tore off the top sheet and drew the line of her jaw, the shape of her eyes, and the slant of her nose. Not a caricature.

"Who are you?" she asked.

"Well, that's a mystery even to me," he answered. "Will you let me paint you? Soon? Here's my card. Now scoot. I've got to earn my keep."

Muffy rose. Peter retrieved the drawing he'd torn from the pad and handed it to her. Staring back at her was the woman intent on Peter's silly story. He had elicited, seen, and captured that interested part of herself. Not the serious Arts Center director, not the social party girl, but the open, curious state of herself she hadn't felt in years.

"Muffy," said Mrs. Roberts. "There's a call for you. Your father."

Chapter Two

Dread and anger replaced the light feeling the artist had conjured. "I'll take it in James's office," she said.

Grasping the caricature in one hand and Peter's card in the other, she turned back toward her friends. They smiled and tilted their heads to see the drawing. She donned her social smile, held the drawing before her like a shield, and twisted her way between them.

How many times had she escaped her father's stern glare and harsh lectures in this old home? After tonight, no more.

She dropped the drawing on the leather sofa and picked up the receiver from James's desk. "I've got it, Glenna," she said. A click signaled her privacy.

"You know I'm hosting a party," she said, seething.

"Alexandra, we have a financial crisis."

Muffy felt snatched from her day and thrown back into that endless whirlpool. The manipulative tapes raced through her mind.

"You drive a new BMW, Alexandra. Shouldn't you show your father some appreciation?"

"I paid for your Wharton MBA, Alexandra. Is this the way you thank me?"

"Father, I'm busy. We will address this tomorrow. Don't

Sublime Recline 9

call here again." She forced herself not to slam the receiver down.

Gritting her teeth, she raised her arms and locked her fingers over her head. Despite the best antiperspirant money could buy, she could imagine sweat marks dipping to the waist of her awful dress.

It was dull and boring, yes. And yes, although it was right for business, it was wrong for a party. She replayed the artist's wide grin and felt an odd warmth in her chest.

Lowering her arms and her eyes, she noticed Leah's open letter on the desk. The gardener was resigning, finished in less than two weeks.

Pieces of the puzzle started to fit. Visions of uncut grass and scraggly flower beds, the artist's mention of a shared employer, gossip about the sale of the estate and the look in James's eyes formed a new picture. There was no place for the shape of Muffy Sergeant.

Sounds from the party dragged her back to the present. Still too disturbed by the call to return to her role as the cheerful hostess, she sank into the leather sofa. Only an empty cushion separated her skin-and-bones self from her charcoal-and-paper self. The gulf between her hostess self and her hidden self was widening.

Looking down at the card crushed between her fingers, she uncurled it and read:

Peter Gant
Portraits and Fine Art

No address. Just a phone number. Pennsylvania, but not local.

Gant. With his fair features, she'd expected an O'Malley or O'Rourke. Maybe Gant was a shortened version of some Irish name. Or maybe it was a name from his childhood, like Muffy.

She had never used Alexandra, her given name. Even her

driver's license read Muffy M. Sergeant. Her nickname was one of the few living gifts she had from her mother. She was named Alexandra Madeleine for both her parents, and her mother had made up a song: "Mommy's Maddy Muffin." It was a secret that the serious Arts Center director kept tucked deep in her heart.

She laid the card in her lap, leaned back against the leather, and unconsciously crossed her arms across her chest. Her fingertips pressed the muscles above her breasts. She had been taught to feel for lumps before she even had breasts. Dr. Sergeant had so instilled the fear of the disease in her that she found herself checking and rechecking more often than she realized.

What are you going to do now, Maddy Muffin? James doesn't want you and, really, you don't want him. If the doctor believes he, or we, have a financial crisis. . . .

Struggling to clear her mind of malpractice suits, her trust fund, and the financial manager she didn't quite trust, she gazed through the corner windows. A sky of scarlet, cherry, fuchsia, and copper carried her thoughts to Peter Gant, Fine Artist.

Does he paint landscapes as well as he paints people? I wonder if he teaches? Would he teach at The Arts Center?

The smile he'd coaxed to her lips came again and relaxed her face and mind. If he were fast and patient and liked squirmy kids. . . .

She rose and set the drawing on the coffee table with the artist's card where she'd retrieve it after "The Talk."

When she returned to the ballroom, it was too loud to think. For the next three hours, she didn't. Years ago, she had developed the ability to compartmentalize her life. She kept school in a safe spot and the horrors of home behind a thick wall. She allowed friends all the room they'd take and gave love the little corner left over. James had been the convenient, expected filler of that corner.

As the servers collected glasses and plates, the guests kept talking and laughing. A good party. A good mix of people.

Good food. Good service. And, she had to admit, Leah had provided good entertainment.

During the evening, Muffy spoke with all her guests, but she always circled back toward Peter. She had hoped to speak with him about teaching—find out where he came from and why she hadn't heard of him.

Not once did he meet her eyes. He seemed so focused on his work that he was oblivious to her or even the party.

Now, he stood studying the Ketches. Katherine sat in the chair; Trevor stood behind her. The evening sun was long set, but Peter seemed to sense his subject's essence without it.

Muffy studied the artist. He stood just as tall as he had hours ago. After his evening's work, he looked invigorated rather than tired. His bronze hair grazed his chin, the ponytail long gone. Part of her wanted to tell him to wait for her; the rest of her couldn't disturb him.

"Bye, Muffy. Thanks."

"Great party."

"Nobody does it better, sweetheart."

"Can you give me the caterer's number?"

All evening Peter had fought with himself to see the cartoon in the figures before him instead of the Muffy in his mind. Although she had fine bones and flawless skin, she had no idea how to make herself beautiful. Why would she pull her hair back from her high forehead? Why wear boring beige?

Yet, in the few moments he'd spent with her, he'd seen a kaleidoscope of expressions. He wanted to capture them all. But. The expressions were part of a real woman. A woman who was in the process of being replaced, whether she knew it or not.

James would not have bought the small painting of Leah and commissioned a portrait if Muffy were the love of his life. And, from the way Leah had described her, Muffy could be vicious. Not the kind of woman Peter needed in his life. Especially now.

He forced his hands to hang at his sides while he searched

the faces of this last couple for their distinguishing traits. He found nothing.

He glanced away and saw Muffy hugging her guests goodbye. As he looked back at his subjects, the perfect couple smiled.

"Can you smile real wide?" he asked.

They complied, revealing their perfect, brightened white teeth.

"Okay, let's try this. Stand up. Face each other. Nose to nose. There."

From the side, his hairline was just a little high, her nose just a little sloped. Neither feature was distinct enough to exaggerate.

"No," he sighed. "Sit back down."

He looked at the blank white page and drew two perfect ovals. Then he surrounded them with a large circle. Using the flat edge of a charcoal stick, he filled the space outside the circle with black.

"Perfection isn't funny," he said, as he tore the page from the pad. "Here's a magic charm to keep the dark from your charmed life."

He nodded as they thanked him, embarrassed that he'd cheated them. Giving them nothing but an art-school exercise, he was angry with himself for being so distracted. Unprofessional.

After the perfect couple had left, Muffy gestured for him to wait while she disappeared down the hall with James. He couldn't. The guests were gone; his work was finished.

He was eager to be in his studio sketching, emptying his head of the myriad images he'd collected this evening. He wanted to sketch Muffy while he could clearly remember her. He hoped she'd tossed his card. He should never have given it to her. But it was an impulse. How could he have known she'd be so distracting?

As Peter closed the easel, James closed the office door.

"Want a drink?" he asked.

"No, thank you," Muffy said.

Sublime Recline

"A seat?" he gestured toward the pair of leather club chairs.

She shook her head. "You're in love with Leah."

He nodded.

"Well, at least I don't have to wait for you any longer."

"I'm sorry, Muffy. I just assumed that we—"

"I assumed too." For the first time in her life, she felt grateful that she wouldn't be spending the rest of it with him.

"What do you know about this Peter Gant?" she asked.

"He's one good artist."

"And?"

James shrugged.

"I need to talk to him. The Strekers need a portrait. You know Becca's sick. And I want him to teach at The Arts Center. Mind if we use the library? I mean, he seems fun and he's obviously talented, but he made a comment about painting me bare. Probably a joke, but I'd feel safer here."

"Sure."

Muffy hurried back to the ballroom. "He's gone!"

She rushed to the door in time to see taillights disappearing behind the giant magnolia.

"Come on," said James. "We'll catch him."

They scrambled into the dark Mercedes and raced down the empty driveway. The only lights they saw on River Road were vanishing around the curve to the north. James soon caught up and flashed his headlights. The car stopped on the shoulderless road.

James turned the lights on bright and joined Muffy as she dashed up to the dark Rolls Royce. Long, charcoal-smudged fingers held an open wallet out the window. Muffy took it and held it in the headlights' glare.

"You're not Peter Cinnsealaigh. You're Peter Gant."

"And you're not a cop." Peter burst from the Rolls.

"No, I'm not." Muffy laughed. "Would you come back to Waite's for awhile? I'd like to discuss some Arts Center business with you."

Peter reached into his tux and removed a large watch. No band.

"I have until midnight and then all of this," he swept his arm back to include his clothes and the car, "turns into pumpkins and rags."

"I don't believe a word of it," said Muffy. "Follow us. We'll turn around at Morgan's. Next drive."

James led them into the nearly empty library at the foot of the stairs. "I hope you'll excuse me, it's been a long day." Turning to Muffy, he added, "Just call if you need me."

"Thanks, James."

The only furniture in the room was an antique red-brocade conversation piece. Around a flat walnut post, three seats were aligned so their occupants could easily see each other's faces and converse.

Muffy loved and hated this sofa. James had teased her, hid from her, lectured her, and once kissed her here. She offered it to Peter.

He glanced up at the chandelier and back to Muffy. He circled the seats. "Could you sit there? Awful light, but I'll work around it."

She perched at the edge of the closest section.

"I've wanted to draw you all night," he said. "It's difficult to draw lips and cowlicks when what I'm really seeing are your ears. Your ears are sculpture. You don't mind, do you?" He opened the pad and his left hand began laying down lines as if they'd been stored in his fingertips.

"My ears?" she murmured. Deciding ears were innocent, she relaxed.

"Have you ever really studied ears?" he answered. "In some, the cartilage looks broken; some are out of proportion. Yours look like a precisely designed maze. Could you turn just a little?"

While he drew, she studied his features. Light copper stubble had grown on his chin and cheeks. His green eyes held an intense, continually astonished look. His mouth was very wide. She pictured it forming long words, generous smiles, and teasing kisses.

Kisses?

Sublime Recline

Muffy clutched the cushion, reassuring herself of the safety of this chair, the house, and James, upstairs.

James had been the only man she'd allowed herself to consider sensually. Tonight she'd moved him to the "friends" compartment of her mind.

She stared at the artist. He stood still as stone except for his left hand. His eyes were focused on her face but she could tell he only saw her surface, as she only saw his. Although his outside was tall, trim, and attractive, she wondered about the inside. Where did that talent come from and how far could it take him? What magic lay beneath that smile?

"Who are you?" she asked. "Peter Gant or Peter Cinn-something-or-other, or are you really Sean O'Malley?"

His merry gaze wrapped her in a peaceful glow. "My all-time favorite shirt is a blue oxford Gant that I picked up at Goodwill for a buck-fifty. Still have it. Sleep in it."

Muffy shivered. She fought the picture of bronze hair escaping from the edges of an open shirt.

"Your mouth's not a classic full," he said. "More lavish. Like you've gathered your lips for a kiss. Of course you haven't.

"You want official nomenclature. Peter Gant, Portraits and Fine Art. I thought that had a concise, professional appearance. Gant. Easy to remember."

"Your pen name."

"How long's your hair?" he asked.

She flicked her chest with her fingers. "Mr. Gant, The Arts Center needs a painting teacher. We have a very strong drama group, but the quality of our art staff is lacking. Do you teach?"

"No."

Her mouth and spirits fell. How could he be so blunt?

"You must," she said. "You describe my ears and mouth. You could at least explain line and proportion. And color. The tints and shades you used to capture Leah were perfect. How do you know Leah?"

"Lovely Leah, garden maid. My landlady's our employer."

"Leah works for James," Muffy corrected.

"Leah's a busy woman."

Muffy remembered the letter she'd seen on James's desk.

"You have the most expressive face," said Peter, his sketching hand at rest.

Muffy flashed him a beguiling smile. "Wouldn't you consider doing a class? Any medium. Any subject. You pick the days and times."

"No." He grinned.

"Why not?"

"Waste of time. Would you rest your hands over each other on the chair arm, and then your head? Like this." He modeled, settling into an empty seat.

The lightest scent of rich cologne settled with him. He leaned back and propped the sketch pad between them.

"Could you rest your hands?" he repeated.

"No."

"Why not?"

"Why is teaching a waste of time?"

"I live in Paoli. I would waste hours traveling and coddling a bunch of rich, old dabblers while they wasted expensive oils on a lousy still life of a lemon that would only collect dust in the basement of the relative who got it for Christmas. Would you take your hair down?"

Disheartened, Muffy knew he was right.

She tipped her head and peered at Peter from beneath her lashes. With both hands, she released the silky, golden strands from the grasp of pins and combed them through her fingers. Assuming the pose he requested, her hair draped over her back.

"Perfect!" His eyes darted over her features. "Except . . . actually, it would be better if you would swing your head and let your hair fall forward."

She lifted her head, flung her hair, and rested her cheek on the back of her hands.

"Almost. Will you do it again?"

She repeated the move faster, then slower.

"There. Thank you."

What am I doing at Waitehaven in the middle of the night letting an artist I've never heard of sketch me?

"Awful dress, but you're gorgeous."

Could he have meant that? Stop it. Don't even think about it. You have waited your whole adult life for James. You are not going to even think about any man until you have all the facts and have analyzed the whole situation.

As she looked back at his eyes, he grinned. Unbidden, uncontrollable, that warmth flooded her heart again.

She took a slow, deep breath so as not to change her pose. "So, is Peter Cinnsealaigh your real name?"

Chapter Three

Muffy awoke to the sound of rain pelting the windows. On the wing chair in the corner of James's guest room, her linen dress lay over Peter's jacket. She lay under the cozy covers for a moment reliving fragments of the past evening.

Peter Cinnsealaigh.

"Ancient Irish surname. My very own. Do you like it?"

She did. She loved the feel of the sounds on her tongue. Softer sounds than Sergeant.

"Was your family Cinnsealaigh Steel?"

He'd acknowledged the connection and changed the subject.

She had thought about leaving, but something in that green-eyed gaze kept her in that chair. She'd tried to stay awake, but some combination of after-party letdown and those dreamy poses relaxed her beyond control.

They had passed much of the night in the library. Most in silence. Sometimes she would startle, awaken, and catch his grin. Another question would bubble to the surface of her mind and escape through her lips.

"Do you have family in Paoli?"

"No. Could you lift your hair from that eyebrow? No, left. Yeah. Is that your mother's nose or your dad's?"

"Mine. Won't you teach just one day a week?"

"Can't. Do you play the flute?"

"Why would you ask?"

"Your mouth. Sometimes you hold your lips as if you're either going to make music or try to keep from yelling."

Her mother had played the flute. She had started to teach Muffy. Peter's question made her wonder where in that vast house her father had hidden it.

That was the pattern of the night. Questions cast out by each of them reeled in words but no answers. His questions opened the dark chamber of her heart where all her wounds and fears were stored. She saw in the flicker of a frown that her questions did the same to him.

He must have left after the storm. She'd awakened beneath the rich scent and silky lining of his jacket. After calling his name, she had walked to the door and peered down the dark drive. Only her car and James's remained. She had turned out the lights and climbed upstairs to the guest room.

Now, she pushed back the old Waite covers and rose into the dreary day. After slipping on her wrinkled dress, she smiled at his coat.

I'll have to return this. See where he lives. See him in daylight. See who he really is.

She tossed the coat over her arm and walked down the grand old stairway. Following the scents of coffee and baking, she found the others in the breakfast room.

"Morning, James, Glenna."

James sat on the chintz-covered wicker at the round breakfast table. The yellow paint, paper, and fabrics usually made the room look sunny, even in the rain. Today it looked dingy.

"Morning, Muffy, there's scones for you and coffee," said the housekeeper.

"You find out what you wanted?" asked James.

"No thanks, Glenna, I've got to get home. I don't know, James. He said he wouldn't teach, but . . . I don't know."

"Well, I'll leave you ladies. River's reaching the hundred-year flood level. When Leah comes, could you send her to the fort?"

"Out in the woods? In this rain?" asked Mrs. Roberts.

"She hasn't melted yet." He smiled over his shoulder.

Muffy watched him leave feeling neither affection nor possession, just a hole in her life. Turning back to Mrs. Roberts she said, "I can remember handing him nails to build that tree fort. And moving rocks in the river to build his dams. You know he's in love with her."

Mrs. Roberts nodded. "We all just assumed. . . ."

"So did I. Stupid. Stupid to wait so long for something so wrong. Thank you, Leah. You can enjoy the flood plains and weirs and retention ponds. I love art. And I've got to get to work."

She left the breakfast nook for the last time and hurried to the office to retrieve her caricature and the mystery man's card.

As she drove into town, Peter's merry grin, sparkling eyes, and flying fingers filled her mind. If he wouldn't teach, she would at least persuade him to show his work at The Center.

It was nearly 8:00 as she parked the red BMW under the portico of the huge white house. Judging by the cars parked beyond the hedge, patients were already waiting for her father in the office of the converted carriage house.

Dr. Alexander Sergeant was the only doctor affiliated with Central County Medical Center who still had his office at home. When his colleagues were consolidating their practices and signing on with HMOs, he had been caring for his dying wife between office hours.

The doctor closed the business section of *The Philadelphia Inquirer* and gently pressed the little mound on the side of his belly. Couldn't be appendix; he'd lost that years ago.

He pushed his chair back from the linen-draped table. Uncovered, the remaining bran muffins cooled in their basket.

"Grace!"

Grace Gazner had been the housekeeper for the Sergeants as long as Glenna Roberts had served the Waites. She closed her pencil in the word-search puzzle book, slapped it on the kitchen table, and sauntered through the back hall. Just before

Sublime Recline 21

she entered the dining room, she saw Muffy walk through the entryway. The young woman's hair hung loose, her dress was wrinkled, and she carried a man's dark coat over her arm. Grace swung her foot back and paused, ready but hidden in the hall.

"And where have you been all night?" growled the doctor.

All the comfortable compartments of Muffy's mind closed. She marched into the dining room, glaring. "You called about a financial problem?"

Craning his neck in exaggerated arcs, he studied her hands. He crossed one long leg over his knee and twisted the giant diamond on his left hand. "I don't care what the rest of your generation does, Alexandra. I expect my daughter to sleep at home until she's wed."

She fought the urge to tell him she had been an adult, and not just his daughter, for years. She could not will the blood from her face or slow her heart, but she would not defend her actions like a child reporting to a parent.

Let him be the fool.

"Is there a financial problem, or did you simply want my attention?" she asked.

He rose and snickered. "I have your attention, dear. First, it's time you put that MBA to use and got a real job. And second, it's time you managed the family finances instead of squandering them."

Me? I live on a salary and trust-fund interest. I don't give half my earnings to a lawyer to bail me out of malpractice suits.

She clamped her teeth together and forced herself to breathe.

He gestured to a folder just past his plate. "There are the statements. They're all gibberish to me, except for one thing: no earnings. You find out what in Hades is going on and fix it! Grace!"

Mrs. Gazner silently retreated three fast steps, stopped, and then bustled from the back hall as if hurrying from the kitchen.

"Doctor?"

"I'm finished here. Don't make lunch." He patted his mouth with the linen napkin, dropped it on his plate, and strode toward the back hall.

Grace stared at Muffy. Muffy glared back. As soon as the back door closed, Muffy scooped up the file and dashed upstairs.

She tossed the file, Peter's jacket, and then her dress and lingerie onto the white canopy bed of her childhood. For a moment she stood naked in the dim light filtering through the white brocade drapes. Then she slipped the dark jacket over her bare body. The tails touched the backs of her thighs and sent a shock of heat from her knees to her cheeks.

"Peter Gant . . . or Cinnsealaigh. Would you keep me waiting for years upon years? You sketch so quickly. Do you live your whole life that fast?"

Don't even think about it. You don't need any men in your life right now. Especially an unknown artist.

She slipped off the jacket and let it rest next to her empty dress, as it had all night, while she dashed into her bathroom for a shower.

Peter emerged from the shower and dried all his bronze hair with a white bath sheet. From an antique walnut chest, he selected a T-shirt, "Millennium Miracle." The last column of a green bar chart blasted over the left shoulder. This business souvenir was from his seven years with AxshunArtz. He pulled it over his head and then stepped into a pair of khaki cutoffs.

Before dashing through his studio and down the stairs of Mrs. Pearlman's carriage house, he set a mug of water in the microwave and pushed the buttons to boil it.

Beneath a green and white golf umbrella, he hustled down the drive. Instead of slick black pavement, he saw Muffy's fine features. He wished there had been a place for her to stretch out. The models he'd sketched and painted in school were mostly students. Young bodies, but not beautiful. Not Muffy.

Even though her arms and legs were long, they weren't bony. As she'd dozed, his gaze had strayed from her face. His pencil had guessed at the hidden curves of that beautiful body.

He'd fought with himself about leaving the jacket. If she knew about James and Leah, she didn't seem to mind. Maybe she was the tough woman Leah had described. Maybe she was the businesswoman she presented to him. She was definitely a model he wanted to paint. He'd left the jacket to force her to call as much as to keep her warm.

Sliding the mail from the box, he tucked it under his shirt. Through the downpour he saw Leah's truck leaving the other side of the circular drive.

"Oh well, Leah. By tonight James will have told you what really happened at the party."

He hustled back and left the umbrella open in the stairway. As he stirred the Folgers instant into the hot water, he sorted his landlady's mail.

"Peter," she had said, "just take the junk and make little origamis out of it. I don't have time for all that begging drivel. But save the garden catalogues."

"*American Artist,*" he mumbled, separating the magazine from the bills and ads. He read "Peter Cinnsealaigh" in the address box. "You crafty old woman. Thank you, Mrs. Pearlman."

He lowered himself to the card table and set his cup on the red heart appliquéd to the corner of the old white bridge cloth.

As a left-hander, he always began a magazine from the back. Between the display ads for watercolor workshops and Italian art schools, classified ads listed competitions and shows by state. There, he found it.

"***Pennsylvania, Philadelphia,*** *'Sublime Recline.' Philadelphia Figure Society's 50th annual juried exhibition, Aug. 4– 19. $4000 Best in Show and other awards. Slides Due: June 26. Entry fee $25/slide. For prospectus send SASE. . . .*"

He dog-eared the page and leafed backward trying to interest himself in Karla Munk's scrawny figures and the garish landscapes of R. T. Quinn. As his focus turned inward, the ads for colored pencils, pastels, and easels blurred into reclining poses of Muffy.

"Sublime Recline," he whispered.

Muffy emerged from her bathroom with one towel around her hair and another around her body. Plucking the ugly dress from her bed, she dropped it down the laundry chute in her closet. In the walk-in, she was surrounded by brown dress after gray suit after Oxford shirt.

It seemed like Dr. Sergeant had chosen and bought them all. Outside the fitting room in Renée Fortier's dress shop, he had sat in the huge leather chair sipping bourbon.

Overriding Renée's fine taste, he'd sneered, "My daughter is a professional woman, Renée. Not a merchant." Then he had lowered his mouth to his glass. "Try the black suit, Alexandra."

Remembering these humiliations, Muffy ripped the French suits and Italian dresses from their padded hangers and threw them into a heap.

A beige linen pantsuit remained at the end of the rod. It would wash out the color in her face, but she had to wear something. She lifted the hanger and brought the outfit to her bed.

My room, but not my home. I always assumed Waitehaven would be my home.

She pictured Leah charging from the river and the woods into the old rooms, wrecking the interior as she'd wrecked the exterior. Then the chaotic vision gave way to James and Leah laughing and cuddling children.

Returning her gaze to her room, she realized it was a girl's room she'd outgrown a decade earlier. For the first time, she began mentally sorting the contents. She turned toward her closet and, rejecting it all, mumbled, "I'll go to Renée Fortier's or Talbots."

Facing the bookcases flanking the windows, she decided to donate the leather-bound classics she'd never opened and business books she'd been told to keep. She would keep only the art books she cherished.

Dressage trophies. Second place. Third place. Did I ever love riding, or was it just something Father thought I should do?

It was fun to ride in the meadows with James. When I was a girl. When I fit this room.

Practicing jumps wasn't fun. Ever. The flute was. So pretty. I wonder what he did with Mother's flute?

She flung the towels on the floor and wrapped herself tight in her white terry robe. Barefoot, she strode down the open hallway and climbed the stairs to the third floor. At the end of the hall, she opened the door to the attic. The hinges creaked and a breath of warm air brushed her cheeks. She hurried up the carpeted steps.

Neat stacks of boxes surrounded sheet-draped chairs. Sunlight pierced the lace curtains on the south wall, but much of the room was in shadow. Working from the far dormer, she searched everywhere for the flute. She found the music stand in the shadow of the chimney by boxes labeled Lenox, Spode, and Sergeant Waterford.

Searching for "Music" or "Madeleine's Flute" scrawled in her father's careless hand, she moved box after box. She pulled lids from long, light, unmarked boxes. Fishing rods.

After straightening the stack she'd sorted, she plodded over to the chairs and lifted a sheet. Her father's old office chair. In its seat lay a black leather case. She crouched down and opened the latches. There, cradled in royal blue velvet, lay the parts of the gold flute.

She lifted and fit each piece into its mate. When it was assembled, she laid her fingers over her mother's fingerprints over the holes.

"Do you play the flute?" he had asked. "You sometimes hold your mouth like you're going to make music. . . ."

"I remember your lessons," she whispered to her mother's invisible ghost. "Why didn't I continue? Couldn't he find another teacher? Couldn't either of us think of the flute without you?"

Carefully, she pulled it apart and returned the pieces to their safe case.

Back in her room, she set the flute case on her bed between the financial folder and Peter's jacket. She opened her lingerie chest and selected the lacy white Victoria's Secret pieces she had bought for herself.

Before her mirror, she touched her lashes with mascara and her lips with pink gloss. Automatically, she worked the mousse into her hair and began to brush it into a sleek knot when she remembered Peter saying, "How long is your hair? Could you take it down? Could you swing it? Could you lift it? Yes!"

The mental tape of Dr. Sergeant's voice interrupted. *"Get that hair out of your eyes. You're a businesswoman. Look like one."*

Muffy took the brush in one hand and the drier in the other. When she finished, sleek gold hung to her chest. She quickly dressed, then scooped up the flute, the folder, and the jacket.

"Grace," she called from the bottom of the stairs.

Over the muffled roar of the dishwasher came the sound of heavy footsteps and an exasperated, "Yes?"

"I've sorted some of my clothes. The ones on the floor of the closet go to Goodwill. Itemize them and get a receipt. I won't be home for dinner."

Chapter Four

The elegant stone mansion on the Haviland estate had been the family's home for generations. Now it housed the office, ballroom, galleries, and classrooms of The Arts Center.

Muffy opened the massive wooden door and slid her umbrella into the ornate Oriental stand just inside. Across the parquet reception area, the door to her office was closed. It had been the pantry. Mr. Haviland's office was too far from the front entrance. The library was perfect for craft and sculpture exhibits. With the addition of just a door and a window, the pantry had become a convenient office for the executive director.

Before Muffy could unlock her office, Niki called out, "Wow! My boss has hair!"

Muffy blushed as she set the flute case, Peter's jacket, and her soft brown leather briefcase on the desk.

"How was the party?" asked the assistant director.

Pictures of Peter vied with those of James, Leah, Heather, and Becca for front row in her mind.

"Fine," she answered, forcing her attention to the present. "Anything pressing this morning?"

Niki handed a yellow Post-it note to Muffy. "Sarah Fox called. Can't teach the figure class for either summer session. Want me to call Wilson?"

"Not yet. Ever hear of Peter Gant?"

"No. You know the dress rehearsal's tonight. And the reception. You're coming, right?"

"Of course."

"Okay, I'll be out in the ballroom if you need me."

Muffy nodded and sank into her chair. *If I really needed you, Mr. Gant, would you teach for me? Do you like plays? Would you come?*

She took his card from the outside pocket of her bag and dialed. After two rings, he answered with an eager smile in his voice. "Peter Gant here."

She smiled. The sound of his voice evoked a picture of his merry eyes. He exuded the happy, excited feeling she always strived to give the guests at her parties.

"Good morning, Peter."

"Muffy! I'll be darned. I was just thinking about you."

She couldn't help beaming. "I have your jacket."

"Yes."

"I'm sorry I was such bad company last night," she said. "Falling asleep and all."

"I put you to sleep," he whispered. "Sleeping models hold perfect poses."

Before she could censor her mind, it filled with a picture of waking and gazing into those bright green eyes. She took a breath and erased it. "We have a dress rehearsal for *Major Barbara* at The Arts Center tonight. Would you come?"

"*Major Barbara?*"

"George Bernard Shaw play about the Salvation Army."

"Oh! *MAJOR Barbara.*"

Silence.

"Peter?"

"Your audience doesn't want to hear my cell phone ringing with your party guests calling for portraits. And, I have other work. Why not come here?"

Silence.

"I have this dress rehearsal," she repeated.

"Are you in it?"

"No, but. . . ." *I have to go. Don't want to go. I've always gone. Don't need to go. Should go. But I really don't have to.* "Where are you?"

He gave her directions to his studio in Paoli, on Philadelphia's Main Line. "Don't eat," he added.

Muffy hung up the phone and then draped his jacket on the brass rack behind the door with her beige cashmere cardigan.

After checking her calendar and returning four calls, she opened the folder from her father. Under the letterhead of Halliday and Crawford Financial Consultants was a statement listing four mutual funds. She didn't have to look at the numbers to see the first mistake. Dr. Sergeant had let his buddy talk him into all front-end-loaded funds. Not that Everest and Richfield didn't have some big winners, but Halliday got his commission up front, regardless of whether the funds earned or lost money.

She turned to the next page. Same funds, same first-quarter statement. She put the sheets side by side. The top sheet was prepared for Dr. Alexander Sergeant. The next was prepared for Dr. Alexander Sergeant, trustee for Alexandra M. Sergeant.

At thirty, Muffy had five years to wait before she could control her trust or withdraw any principal. Heart pounding, hands shaking, she turned page after depressing page in the folder.

"My God, did he give them everything?"

She examined the certificates of deposit redeemed early, money market accounts closed, and the conservative, dividend-paying bond funds sold. He had transferred all the proceeds to the greedy, inept Halliday and Crawford to invest in formerly prosperous funds.

She put her trust-fund report back on top and gasped. The ending balance was thousands below that of the start. No earnings at all last month.

Muffy's head pounded. Slamming the folder shut, she shoved it into her briefcase, picked three aspirin tablets from the tiny cloisonné box in her bag, and trudged to the kitchen.

Niki was sorting an inventory of colored candles. One glance at Muffy and she gasped. "What happened?"

"I need a drink."

"Oh dear, wine's not here yet. But there's scotch and gin in the cupboard. Let me get the key."

"No," said Muffy. "Just water." She opened the fridge and withdrew a bottle of Perrier. One sip after she swallowed the aspirin, she choked. Amid coughs, wide eyes, and waving arms, she blurted, "Halliday. Halliday and Crawford. The endowment." She stared deep enough into Niki's eyes to fully transmit her panic.

A bewildered Niki asked, "What? He's a board member—treasurer."

Muffy took a deep breath trying to compose herself, trying to resume her role as executive director, trying to cram terrified Maddy Muffin back into her own compartment in her mind. If Halliday had put all the Sergeant money in the same four funds, he'd probably put The Arts Center's money there too.

"Have we received a financial statement this month?" she asked.

Niki shook her head. "Henry presents that at board meetings. I don't know where he keeps the papers."

Lightning flashed and the crash of a giant tree competed with the thunder. A new torrent of rain pelted the old windows. Muffy let the storm suck the turbulent energy from her head.

Abruptly, fluorescent bright switched to daylight dim. Thunder crashed again.

"Miss Sergeant?" Consuela called from the entry. She and her husband, Juan, lived in the gardener's cottage behind the mansion in exchange for taking care of The Center, inside and out.

Muffy marched toward the voice with Niki behind her.

"The tree, ma'am. He is down."

Muffy peered out the high bay window at the giant tulip tree resting on two Mercedes and blocking the exit for all the students and teachers whose classrooms were now without light.

"Thank you, Consuela. Does Juan have his chainsaw?"

"In the truck, I think."

"When the storm passes," asked Muffy, "can he . . . ?"

"Yes, ma'am. We cut it up. We have the wood?"

"Of course." She turned to Niki as the first students appeared on the great stairway. "Serve them ice water in the ballroom. Talk up the play. Consuela, set up tables with candles. I'll call the insurance agent."

Muffy trudged to her office and closed the door. Barbara Burton would laugh and buy an even bigger car. Helen Latimore would call her lawyer from Muffy's office.

Niki's offer of scotch or gin sounded better and better as the wretched day progressed and the throbbing in her head intensified. Peter hadn't had to tell her not to eat. There had been no time.

Skirting the puddles on the way to her car, she tried to shut out the sight of tree debris and fallen foxgloves. The play and garden party were always scheduled for this June weekend when the grounds were at their best.

Now, she would have to pay Consuela and Juan extra to clean it up. How much money The Center had for unbudgeted expenses, she had no idea. Although she helped prepare the annual budget, she left the investments to Halliday and the bookkeeping to Niki.

Wedged in rush-hour traffic, she locked her financial fears away and opened the mental door to Peter Gant. A smile relaxed her face. For the next hour, she basked in fresh memories and fantasies safely hidden from Dr. Sergeant's criticism and control.

When she parked in the center of Mrs. Pearlman's crescent drive, she was impressed. Beneath the storm's litter of leaves and limbs, the grounds were perfect. Perfectly cut grass led to perfectly trimmed boxwood bordering a brilliant white Victorian mansion. A sunroom on the left balanced a conservatory on the right. "I guess Leah the garden wrecker can make a place look beautiful."

She saw the Waite estate from a new perspective and felt her first moment of sympathy for Leah. Since Muffy had been such a part of that place, she had never noticed how neglect had destroyed its beauty.

"Hi!"

She turned to see Peter striding barefoot through the wet grass. His smile released her headache and warmed her heart.

"Good afternoon," she said.

Peter glanced at the sun dangling at the treetops. "Let's call it evening," he corrected with mischief in his eyes. He stopped, cocked his head, and waved for her to follow as he dashed toward the carriage house.

Muffy stood dazed before she heard the phone he was running to answer. For a moment, she wanted to be Maddy Muffin and fling off her shoes and trouser socks and run barefoot through the grass. Ms. Sergeant, MBA, would fetch her bag and briefcase, lock the car, and march along the drive.

Escaping both selves, Muffy left her bags in the car and her shoes on the pavement. The wet grass cooled her feet and soaked her socks. She glanced at the long, white porch with its white, wicker chairs. Wandering toward the carriage house, she noticed a row of staked lilies hugging its side.

"Pretty," she murmured. "Very pretty."

Her mind leapt back to the memory of her childhood home. When her mother and Vivienne Waite were best friends and gardeners, her own home was as lovely as this. After her mother died, the doctor had the flowers replaced with pachysandra and hired a service to cut the grass and trim the privet hedge.

She turned and studied Peter's home. The weathered, cedar-shingled building had wide swing-out doors below and big new windows above. Over the door where Peter had vanished, a small stained-glass window caught the afternoon sun.

A wave of relaxation passed through her like a fine screen,

sifting out Mrs. Latimore's threats, the financial mess, and the last of her headache.

Strolling closer, she heard him thunder down the stairs. He burst through the doorway with a million-dollar smile. "A commission! Heather Chandler wants a family portrait. Four generations."

Muffy remembered her promise and chided herself for not checking her file of artists. She'd thought about asking Peter last night, but she didn't know him. He'd answered her questions in circles. It was better that Heather had called him herself.

"She's my oldest friend," said Muffy. "We spent summers at their cottage in Rehoboth Beach."

"Yeah," said Peter. "She wants me to come for a week, or as long as I need." Dimples framed his smile. His eyes twinkled. "Come on up."

While memories of sailing, sunburns, and sand castles jostled with images of strolling a sunset beach with Peter, she followed him through the colored light cast onto the stairs through the stained glass.

At the top, she turned into an open room of bright white walls and dark oak floors. In the center, an old wooden easel held a huge canvas of Leah and a table filled with jars of brushes, tubes of paint, and a plastic box big enough to hold a sheet cake.

Muffy imagined the finished portrait hanging in the dining room at Waitehaven. Unconsciously, she sighed. She'd always imagined her own portrait there. This was one more adjustment she would have to make to the self that, yesterday, had seemed so set and solid.

Notes of Bach filled the room. "My studio." Peter held his long arms wide.

Looking at him, her whole life seemed like a dim memory. She smiled. "Congratulations on your commission. You'll have a great time with the Strekers. I still think of her as a Streker. If I had a glass, I would toast your brilliant career."

He grinned, vanished into the adjoining room, and returned with a bottle of merlot and two wineglasses. She watched him set them on the table with his painting supplies and retrieve a corkscrew from his pocket. His long fingers grasped the metal handle and expertly twisted the screw into the cork until it vanished.

Like a well-trained waiter, he offered her a splash to test. She waved her hand and he filled both glasses.

"Here's to your success," she said. "May it grow continually and take you to the top of the international art world." She tapped her glass to his. Their eyes remained locked as the wine wet their lips.

"And here's to you, beautiful Miss Muffy, my model. I hope."

Muffy cocked her head, looked into those dazzling green eyes and extended her arm. As he tapped his glass to hers, their fingers touched. Warm.

He'd intended to simply tap the glass again, but with that open look in her eyes, that outstretched, offering arm, he let the backs of his fingers rest against the backs of hers.

Not intending to, not planning to, desperately wanting to, mentally shouting at himself not to, he slowly bent, gazing into her eyes all the while, giving her every chance to move, to laugh, to push him away, to say, "Not now, Peter, not yet."

She didn't. He slowly sank into the swell of her soft, inviting lips.

Realizing she had been pulled to this moment from the moment she'd seen him appear at the party, she tipped her head, offered her lips, and closed her eyes to the tingling sensation. Although only their lips touched, she felt the warmth of his kiss race through her body from her mouth to her toes.

When he drew away, she opened her eyes. For the first time, he looked serious.

"I didn't intend to do that," he said through heavy breaths.

She gazed at him in wide-eyed astonishment. "Neither did I."

Peter looked down at her inviting mouth and felt torn be-

Sublime Recline 35

tween wanting to feel her lips again and wanting to sketch their fullness. As the man overcame the artist, his empty arm reached around her shoulder and drew her close.

The woman he held and tasted was neither the cool socialite he'd sketched at Waitehaven, nor the hard-hearted snob Leah had described. This one was dangerous. This tender, sensuous soul could steal his heart without even trying.

He released her and backed away.

"You kiss as well as you paint," she whispered.

"Ah, I have food," he said. "In here."

He led her through the archway to his spotless, bare-bones kitchen, dining, living room. On the cloth-covered card table, he'd set two places of Wedgwood china.

Muffy stood bewildered as Peter withdrew an assortment of bowls from the fridge. He removed the covers, revealing combinations of shrimp, pasta, fruits, vegetables, herbs, and oils.

Her director self wanted to take over and arrange the food. Her curious self stood and watched the man's graceful movements. She drew her bottom lip inside her mouth to see if the taste of his kiss remained.

Leave. Just leave now. Don't get involved. You don't know anything about him.

Her stomach growled.

He heard and grinned. "You're wonderful," he said. "I ask you to take down your hair and you do. I ask you not to eat, and you don't."

With a shiver, she wondered what else he might ask her to do. And why, when she was always the one in control, was she doing what he asked?

I couldn't eat, and taking my hair down is no big deal.
But you left it down, didn't you?
Who on earth is he?

She searched the glass cabinet and bare counters for clues to the real Peter. All she saw was an open magazine.

"Would you have a seat?" he asked.

"Thank you."

As she spooned minted fruit, dilled cucumbers, and Thai

salad onto her plate, he set a basket of tiny orange muffins between the serving bowls.

"I'd warm them," he said, "but all I have is a microwave and that wrecks them."

"Where do you find the time for gourmet cooking around your art?" she asked.

"My friend, Thea. You don't mind leftovers do you? Thea's a caterer. Actually, they aren't real leftovers. She's trying new recipes. Hey, you'd know better than me. You must eat tons of. . . ." He smiled that warm smile again. "You obviously don't eat tons of anything, but you probably eat catered food more often than I do. Is it okay? Is it different from the stuff you usually get? Thea wants distinctive food. I like it, but I wouldn't know."

"She shouldn't try to be too different. People want safe, familiar, fresh, and delicious. Do you have her—never mind." Muffy dropped her eyes and raised her fork to her mouth.

Peter took a sip of wine. "So," he said, "you don't have the authority to choose the caterer, or you won't be needing one?"

Muffy plucked a muffin from the basket and broke it in two. "I have the authority," she answered.

He watched an icy composure harden her features. *This must be the Muffy Leah knows. If this is the real Muffy, I've got a chance.*

He let the silence build between them. Better not to know what complications sizzled in that mind. Too bad his heart did not agree with his head.

She grasped the stem of the goblet with her delicate fingers. Her guarded gaze met his. "There are some financial matters I need to clear up," she said.

Chapter Five

Peter had some financial matters of his own to clear up. AxshunArtz had paid his student loans and much, much more. The bonuses and promotions had seduced him into staying two years longer than he'd planned.

Now he had to convince Glen Rossiter, the financial manager who'd negotiated the sale of the game company, to leave the money where it was and stay away from stocks. He didn't care about growing his wealth; all he needed was a modest, but guaranteed, income.

And a model. Could he paint her for the contest without falling in love with her? With the new commission, he wondered when he'd find the time. But, he knew he would. When he painted, he didn't need food or sleep. He needed a model. He tried not to want Muffy. The soft, sleepy Muffy from last night. Or the kissable Muffy from moments ago.

"What are you reading?" she asked.

Peter turned and saw the *American Artist* folded to the page of the figure contest.

"An art magazine. Seems Mrs. Pearlman bought me a subscription. Came today."

"You have so much talent," she said. "Do they have articles about managing your career? I mean promotion and pricing?"

Peter remembered that after he'd read the contest posting,

he'd only skimmed the rest of the magazine. He could remember neither names nor products, headlines or pictures. All he could see were Muffy's long limbs, stretched out on a chaise, and her beguiling eyes peeking through that silky golden hair. He longed to see the curves of her bare arms and the arch of her foot. As he imagined her in pose after pose, he understood how Andrew Wyeth could paint Helga over and over and over.

"I didn't get a chance to read it," he finally answered.

"Our figure instructor cancelled for the summer sessions," she said.

His mind raced. Images of Muffy reclining beneath a gauzy drape replaced the image of sitting in traffic on the way to The Arts Center.

"But maybe that's a good thing," she said. "We may need to cut back anyway."

Peter tried to give it some thought. If his mouth had been full, he'd have had time to think. But, no.

"We'll barter," he said. "I'll teach one class if you'll pose for one painting."

Muffy smiled. "Thank you. Class is nine to noon on Wednesdays. Big class. Any medium. I was going to have a model. Can't afford that now." She frowned.

"Why don't you model?" he asked.

She neither blushed nor smiled. "No time. No experience. And I am not going to whip off my clothes for students I know."

"But you'll model for me?"

"Not nude."

"No," he said. "Of course not."

As he began clearing the table, the sinking sun glinted off the light copper hairs on his arm. Muffy surreptitiously watched, recalling the strength of that arm and the tenderness of his kisses. She chewed the last bite of minted fruit.

"Tell your friend," she said, "that Thai is good, but make it mild. The fruit's perfect. Crisp, fresh, delicate dressing. The shrimp is boring, overdone. Different's fine, but stay away from bizarre.

"Thank you for dinner, Peter. I've got to run to make that reception."

He whirled around. "No. Don't go yet. I have dessert."

She held up her hand and gave him her practiced dismissal smile.

"Thank you so much, but I couldn't eat another bite." She glanced for her bag, then remembered she'd left it in the car. Along with her keys. Not like herself.

"Well, let me see you out," he said. "Did you bring my jacket?"

Her faced warmed. She felt like little Maddy Muffin standing at her mother's bed without the ice water she'd been asked to bring.

Peter's laugh filled the room. "You have the most expressive face I've ever seen. I could paint you for the rest of my life and still not capture every nuance. If I'm not careful I'll be as obsessed with you as Dali was with Gala."

Muffy stood dumbstruck listening to this confession. Last night she'd have been flattered. Last night his joy would have been contagious. Now she knew the kiss had been a bribe. Like the teaching was a bribe. He saw her only as an object to paint. At least her time-tested escape was ready and waiting. A party. Plenty of people. Plenty of details to attend to.

She refocused on Peter, intending a brusque good-bye. No good. If she stayed in his gaze one more second, she would be grinning and flirting, drawn into his manipulative net. Hardly a professional woman.

She turned her wrist to read her diamond-framed Rolex: 7:10.

Yes. Back by eight. Change. Check tables. Watch final scene. Yes. Nab Halliday if he's there. Yes.

With all the seriousness she could muster and her most formal smile, she said, "Come about eight-thirty on Wednesday and I'll show you around. I'll be the lemon in your still life after five. At The Center. Will you need your jacket before that?"

"No, but . . ."

Openmouthed, he watched her rush through the studio. Heard her race down the stairs. From the window, he followed the bright, red car as it slipped out of view. His first impulse was to reach for the pad and pencil and sketch the light shoes abandoned on the black pavement. Instead, he stood staring at the landscape. He saw only an animated sequence of her expressions.

Chris, his partner at AxshunArtz, would see her as a kick-butt monster slayer. Peter fought the years of seeing the world in terms of good and bad guys and landscapes to escape.

By the time she reached home, Muffy had finished berating herself for forgetfulness and romantic assumptions. The only light in the house shone from the first-floor corner window. The den. She hated that room. Forbidden space. "Daddy's reading, don't disturb him. It's medical journals, Muffin. Daddy's got to keep up. Don't disturb him."

But when Maddy's Muffin was less than perfect, Daddy had plenty of time to lecture, patronize, and insult her in his private space. Later, he'd called her to that room to instruct her how to check, make sure the dreaded cancer was not invading the body of his only child.

Tonight, she parked her car under the portico and quietly, she thought, slipped in the back door.

"Alexandra."

She ignored him and hurried up the back stairs on silent, silk-covered feet.

She shut her bedroom door and flipped on the light. It was not the mess she'd left. All the clothes she'd sorted and left on the floor for Goodwill were back on their hangers in the closet.

"Maybe that's a good thing for now, since who knows how I'd replace them."

She stood in the closet and wondered what to wear to the dress rehearsal reception.

"Background music. Let the actors strut. I've always been the background music. Behind the scenes. Making things run smoothly. Well, they may not be running so smoothly now."

"Get a real job," echoed in her mind. She knew what her father meant. Her education and experience demanded a job paying three times her salary. Until now, the money hadn't mattered. Until now, The Center had coasted. Now, for the first time, she felt herself losing control in one part of her life after another.

Better to direct the change than react to it. If I have time.

She snatched a silk dress from the rod as he rapped on the door.

"I'll be down in a minute," she called. "In the dining room."

"In my office," he corrected.

She sighed and trudged to the shower. As she washed, she unconsciously struck poses for the painter. Realizing what she was doing, she shook her head and rinsed.

With her wet, moussed hair wound tight in a bun and her body covered in cocktail clothes, she entered the office with the folder. It was dim, as always. The low-watt globes of the ceiling light were inadequate to rescue the room from twilight. His desk lamp shone only on the open patient files before him.

"You reviewed the statements?" he asked.

"Yes. Basically, it's an asset allocation problem. Someone put all the money—yours, mine, and probably The Arts Center's—into four funds comprising the same stocks. They were good funds, but not now. Halliday has his commission. It doesn't matter to him if the funds gain or lose."

Dr. Sergeant's face was placid. Muffy might have told him three plus four equals seven. He merely stared at her, waiting.

"We need to take at least half of the money out and reinvest it in high-yield bonds where it will generate income for us to live on. You can use the commission as a deduction on the taxes. Same with the loss on the sale of shares."

He closed the top patient file and gave Muffy a sidelong glance. "The other options are?"

Muffy was speechless. Hadn't he heard a word? Did he still trust Halliday? He would never admit he'd made a mistake.

"Options?" she asked. "Leave the money where it is and I'll sue for mismanagement of my trust. Give me control of my money and drum up some needless surgeries. Go tell Halliday he's a stupid thief and he needs to give you all the money back or his name will be . . . let's use a nice medical term . . . feces. I'm going to The Arts Center now. Dress rehearsal reception. Maybe our friend Henry Halliday will be attending. Are you?"

He shook his head.

Muffy set the file on the corner of his desk and strode out the door.

Cars filled the area fronting the old mansion and overflowed into the new theater lot. As she parked in her reserved slot, she looked for Halliday's white Lexus. She found it parked closest to the theater.

She hurried up the steps and thrust open the Center's door. Golden glass wall sconces cast a warm glow over the polished parquet floors and creamy satin drapes. Muffy paused. During her workdays, the place bustled with public activity. On her rare evening visits, she glimpsed the private, quiet state of the original home. Striding down the Persian runner to the ballroom, the silence followed her.

She imagined Peter's presence here. Imagined him upstairs in the big painting room. Sitting in her office. Kissing her on the wide window seat at the top of the stairs.

Stop right there.

She turned off her thoughts as she turned the knob of the ballroom doors. Servers stood in a black and white knot of laughter. She nodded to them, retreated, and closed the doors.

Why am I even here? Niki's got it all under control. I should go out to the theater. Put in an appearance backstage.

She remembered Halliday's car and hardened. After unlocking her office door, she switched on her antique *Gone*

With the Wind lamp. In the glow from its iridescent pink globes, she saw a short note.

Dear Miss Sergeant,
 Juan and me, we move to Kennett Square with family. Too lonely live here. We go next weekend.
 Your true, Consuela
 Maybe we keep job. Part time.

"All right."

Muffy envisioned Juan's old white pickup truck piled with furniture, parked in front of the cottage. A grinning Peter stood at the threshold waving them a merry good-bye.

From the kitchen, she heard commotion signaling the start of the reception. She let her face fill her familiar social mask, closed her office, and began to sort through the crowd for the treasurer.

Chapter Six

When she cornered Henry Halliday, his eyebrow twitched as he agreed to meet her for lunch at Eagle's Nest, the golf course near The Arts Center. "I'll be brief," she said. "Please bring The Arts Center financial statements."

She saw the grimace through his agreeable facade.

Long after the last guests had left, Muffy sat at her computer comparing the yields of CDs, money markets, and bond funds. They were all low, but at least not losing. Her research was a fair distraction, but Peter's grin kept appearing in her mind like the pop-up Internet ads for car loans and classmates.

Now alone in the huge center, she listened to the night sounds unique to every building. Peering through the back windows, she saw the lights in the caretakers' cottage. She imagined stretching on a long sofa hidden behind dark, paneled walls and white, cotton curtains. There, Peter held her instead of his pencil. In that imagined room, she could feel his warmth and relive that kiss again and again.

"I didn't mean to do that." Was that true? And even if it weren't, is there really any harm in spending time with a man who's fun for a change?

And he'll teach. Then I can find out who he really is. Or can I? He always controls the conversation and only half answers my questions.

And even worse, when I'm with him, I don't care.

She shut her computer down, turned out the light, and walked to the back patio doors. Outside, it was so dark she could barely follow the little slate stepping stones through the grass to the cottage. Juan answered her knock with the blue-gray glow of the TV behind his white T-shirt.

"Oh, Miss Sergeant. Come in."

"No, no. Thank you. I got your note. Sorry you're leaving." She glanced past him, mentally replacing the cotton-print, slip-covered furniture with Peter's easel and drafting table and her own imagined sofa.

"Wanted you to know," she continued. "I may be working late for a few days. So the lights you see are mine. Good night."

She turned away.

Peter turned between soft, white sheets. His left hand twitched as his dreaming mind sketched full lips and firm limbs. His model reclined on a lemon-colored cloth draped over a sofa set on a stage. He couldn't see her. People kept passing between them. Real people, like buddies at Glen Mills School for Boys, and Northrop Kingston, his perfectionist monitor at PAFA, the Pennsylvania Academy of the Fine Arts. Fake people like the actor in the doctor costume. Real people like Leah. And fake people like Kleevo the video monster he'd created.

He walked toward the stage, stood in the orchestra pit, and looked up at her. At last, he had a clear view to finish his sketch. He squinted to see the curve of her belly, but her body from her knees to her neck was just a hollow rectangle.

"Here, Peter," said Muffy, the model. "Here's a little still life for you." In her hollow self, she set a bowl of lemons. Then she rose and left the still life in the rectangular space. She laughed at him and peered through her lashes. "See, I am just lemons inside." She walked off the stage, counting the bills in the wad of money she carried.

* * *

While Peter dreamed, Muffy carried the flute to the top of The Arts Center's beautiful curved oak stairway. There, a broad bay window overlooked the patio, lawn, and meadow beyond. Below the window, white cushions padded a wide seat.

She set the flute case on the cushions and opened it. The pieces felt cool as she fit them together. Bringing the assembled instrument to her mouth, she pressed her lips into the position Peter had described as "going to make music or keep from yelling."

She drew a breath, pressed the keys beneath her fingers, and blew. A high clear note filled the hall. She shivered. That note brought back the memories of her mother's smile, her approving nod and gentle hugs.

Muffy closed her eyes, took another breath, and blew as she lifted each of her fingers. Not a scale. Not a song. Just flute notes. Clear and bright.

Suddenly, her fingers and lips remembered the simple, beginner's song her mind had long forgotten, Bach's "Country Garden." She played it slow, then fast, loud and then soft. The dark space echoed with gentle, ethereal notes. The song evolved into a melody of her own. Lost in the tones, she played until her arms grew tired.

She wanted more music. More skill. Soon. After this money mess was resolved. After she had escaped the control of Dr. Sergeant. She pulled the flute apart and set the pieces back into the case.

The Friday morning sun glared into the Sergeant dining room. Muffy lifted the napkin from the bran muffins. Warm. There was no scent of baking in the air.

"All I have is a mircrowave and that wrecks them." Grace doesn't care about wrecking food.

"Grace," she called.

As she waited for the woman to come from the kitchen, she gazed into her favorite painting. Her first art purchase.

The summer her mother died, Jake Waite took her and

James to an exhibit at The Arts Center. After she saw that painting, she'd stood mesmerized and refused to look at any other. Insisted on buying it.

It was not great art. Just an illustration. Nothing she'd buy now, but the realistic people filling the rooms of a fantasy dollhouse had captivated her.

She had spent many lonely meals imagining herself snuggled in the enormous bed with five sisters all eating cookies from a huge basket.

As she grew older, she saw herself as the woman draped in diamonds and silks, laughing with friends in the ballroom. That picture she'd used as a template for her life. Even if she would never have sisters, she had become the elegant hostess.

"Yes," said Grace.

"These muffins aren't fresh."

"Your father wants them."

"I'll have yogurt and fruit. Please."

Grace returned to the kitchen. Muffy heard her father's heavy footfalls on the stairs.

"Morning, Alexandra."

"Morning, Father."

He pulled out his chair and sat.

Grace appeared with coffee and *The Inquirer*. The doctor didn't move until she left.

"Why didn't you tell me about James and the gardener?" he asked.

"You had more important business on your mind."

Grace returned with a bright yellow bowl filled with vanilla yogurt and sliced strawberries. Dr. Sergeant split a muffin and opened the paper.

Muffy gazed past him into the painted house. Another favorite room held artists dressed as jesters. Each aimed a brush at a canvas set on an easel.

Niki will have to call the students in the figure class. Tell them about the change. But what can we say? Mystery artist fills in?

She waited until after 9:00 to call him. She tried not to

imagine waking him, but that bare bronze arm kept reaching out from under a white sheet in her mind.

"Peter Gant here."

"Actually, Mr. Gant, you are far from here."

"Muffy! You're not a lemon."

Don't tease me, Mr. Gant. I can deal with the reality, whatever it is.

"Right. I'm calling... we need to tell the figure students about their new teacher and I know nothing about him."

"PAFA, magna cum. Video game designer. No. That sounds so commercial. Just say PAFA."

"Magna cum? Video games?"

"Student loan payback."

His voice dropped to a whisper. "Could you come here tomorrow? There's this contest. I'd like to make some sketches. I know you said Wednesday, but there's a deadline."

Muffy couldn't breathe. His real voice was so much richer than the memory in her mind.

No. No. Just say no.

"What time?" she asked.

"Breakfast."

"No. The garden party's tomorrow. Noon to three."

"Then come at four. And don't bring shoes. I've got a pair I think will fit you."

With a glass of warm iced tea in his right hand and a tiny brush in his left, Peter never heard Leah's truck. Nor did he hear her knock.

"Peter?"

"Yeah?"

"You okay?"

"Leah?"

"Can I come up?"

"No. I'll come down. Want a drink?"

"No thanks," she said. "Hurry up. I want to show you."

He stepped back and squinted at the oil-painted Leah.

Yes. Check the glints in her hair in sunlight.

He raced down the stairs, hands still full. "Come out in the sun," he said. "Yeah. Burnt sienna, cad yellow. Mmm, nope, scarlet."

Leah spread both hands over her face. She peeked between her fingers, then swished her hands like windshield wipers.

"Wow! Where'd you find that?" asked Peter.

"I can't remember his name," she beamed. "Some jeweler James knows."

"Mr. Waite, himself? You're engaged?"

"Yes!"

Peter whistled. "Wow! Congrats. Then Mrs. P is out of a gardener."

"Not yet," said Leah. "Let me tell her, give her my notice when she gets back. Are you painting? Any calls from the party?" Light sparkled from her huge diamond.

"Yeah. Family portrait. Friend of Muffy's."

Leah tilted her head but let the question remain in a sly smile.

Peter grinned back. "Gotta paint her. Gotta finish you first though. Turn your head a little, huh? Yeah. Rose madder. Who'd have thought? Gotta go. Yell if you need anything, but don't come up. It's a surprise." He winked and vanished back into the carriage house.

Henry Halliday kept Muffy waiting for ten minutes. Normally, she would have paced and muttered. Instead, she relaxed in the leather wing chair, watching golf balls drop onto the ninth green. In a dreamy state, she imagined Peter's green-eyed gaze as he studied the planes of her face.

How do I get him to notice me when I already have his undivided attention? I'll have to work on that.

PAFA? Magna cum laude? Why would he stoop to drawing gorillas and crashing cars? Did he draw Marios or mah-jongg tiles?

"Muffy," said Halliday. It was the first time she had ever wanted anyone to address her as Alexandra. She rose and offered her hand to shake.

"Hello, Henry."

As she turned to follow the hostess to a window table, she noticed he'd come empty-handed.

No problem. Or if there is a problem, as I suspect, we'll just air it at the board meeting.

Halliday cultivated a roundness that invited everyone from grandchildren to CEOs to confide in him with no fear of hitting a sharp edge. Muffy now knew he concealed the equivalent of machetes behind that condescending smile and those too-clean nails.

She matched his martini with ice water and punctuated his local gossip with, "Really?" and "No way." She ate her Somerset salad while he devoured a massive Dagwood burger.

The conversation remained focused on horses and sports cars, conspicuously avoiding the stock market and even the local mushroom-growing business.

"Dessert?" asked the waiter taking her plate.

"No thank you," she answered.

Without listening to Halliday's order, she glanced at her watch and then opened her briefcase. She set the sealed, white envelope where her plate had been, pushed out her chair, and crossed her legs.

"According to my calculations, Henry, even a three percent, front-end load on my trust fund and my father's estate would buy a fully-equipped Lexus. But your commission on Everest and Richfield is four percent, isn't it?"

"Muffy," he laughed and wiped his mouth. "A girl your age is bound to get excited when she sees a little blip in the market."

"Do boys your age put all their eggs in one basket?"

She watched the eyebrow twitch above the concealed grimace.

"You are certainly nothing like your mother, Muffy."

Oh, but I am, Mr. Halliday. In a musical way I remembered only last night.

"No dear, you may have her face, but inside, she was a lady."

"Then that, Mr. Halliday, must make me a gentleman. Under the circumstances, I'll take that as a compliment."

Steel replaced her sneer as she handed him the envelope. "You will get the papers to my father for his signature and transfer funds before the market closes today. I've faxed copies of this letter to my father and our attorney. Since you forgot The Arts Center's papers, you can bring them to an executive committee meeting Monday night."

As the waiter delivered Halliday's cheesecake, Muffy rose. "Thank you so much for a lovely lunch, Mr. Halliday." She flashed him a quick smile, picked up her briefcase, and strode from the room.

Chapter Seven

Muffy loved the garden party even more than the gala in May. It was one of the few occasions a woman could still wear a hat, and it delighted her to see jewelry sparkle in the sunlight.

In a few hours, the back terrace would be filled with linen-draped tables strewn with damask-rose petals. Had she allowed herself to sit, she would have savored tiny watercress or cucumber sandwiches, bites of cake, and sips of punch.

She would have shopped like the members and guests from bright Costa Rican carts filled with items like hand-thrown pots, sweet-grass baskets, and handmade paper notecards.

Just before 9:00, Evelyn Richardson, board member, art critic, and chair of the party, arrived with Neiman Marcus bags filled with rose blossoms.

"Muffy, did you order enough water? You know many people prefer water to punch in this weather. And what about fans? Robert uses a fan on the patio. Did you order fans?"

"Good ideas," said Muffy. "I'll make some calls."

The afternoon sun was warm, but not blazing. Her friends came dressed in their finest, sharing everything from local gossip, stock market tips, and condolences about James. They ran out of punch, water, and pottery but had a few leftover sandwiches and sweet-grass mats. A perfect afternoon. Muffy nearly forgot about her financial problems, but little remarks about the mystery artist kept slipping from her lips.

"Teaching the figure class. PAFA, magna cum."

"Painting the Strekers. All four generations."

"Wants me to pose!" She laughed.

When she was satisfied that Consuela was managing the cleanup, Muffy left. As she relaxed into the black leather seat and navigated the Blue Route traffic to Paoli, Peter slid one huge white sofa in Mrs. Pearlman's living room into every possible light. None was right. Nor would a white background offer enough contrast to Muffy's pale skin. He slid the sofa back to its place.

Usually, he rushed through the upstairs checking windows, lights, and outlets, making sure her house was safe and sound during her absence. This afternoon, he checked spreads of gold satin and quilts of bright prints.

Try as he might to picture Muffy, the model, reclining on a bed or chaise lounge, she kept appearing as Muffy the woman: her full lips parted and her delicate lashes closed.

She's a model, Peter the Gant. Not a lemon; not the love of your life.

Yet, whispered a voice buried so deep in his mind that he barely heard it.

Finding nothing he could use for a background upstairs, he strolled down to the sunroom. Here, he had sketched Leah until he knew every curl of her hair and plane of her face. Here, the light was silky. Like a photographer snapping a 360-degree panorama in sections, he judged each angle, each wall.

"There, right there."

Late afternoon. Backlight. Sublime. A drape. What will I use for a drape? To win, I've got to have everything, plus.

A red flash drew his eye.

She shut the car door as he shut the front door.

"Now I understand," she called. "You only pretend to be the poor artist living in the carriage house. Really, you live in the big house and only use the carriage house for your studio."

Grinning, he strolled barefoot over the grass to greet her. "Great idea," he said. "But not yet."

She stood still, willing herself to be objective. Ask questions. But all she could do was bask in the warmth of his smile and long for another kiss he claimed he hadn't intended.

"It's so good to see you," they said together and then laughed.

Without an invitation, he caught her in his arms and hugged her to his chest. She wrapped her arms around his solid body but kept her head tucked beneath his chin, not trusting herself to look up.

He kissed her hair and released her. She looked up into his serious eyes.

"Sorry," he said. "I wasn't thinking. Just glad to see you. How was the party?"

"Perfect."

"I suppose you've eaten."

"Not a bite. I was so busy with everything. So good to see all my friends." She couldn't help smiling. "I wound up telling them all about you. Like I know so much." She wanted to joke but her mouth wouldn't cooperate. It fell serious and silent. Her eyes asked the questions he didn't answer.

"It's so hot out here," she finally said.

Peter, the man, stared down into her eyes. "And in," he whispered and then laughed. "I forgot to turn the air conditioner on."

Peter, the artist, took over. "Would you come inside for a minute? I want to check out the light. Try a pose."

Muffy stared at him, totally aware of the shift. At least there was a man who shared that head with the artist. She had to find a way to coax him out.

"Sure," she said.

Following him across the grass toward the white porch, she studied the loose way he moved and his large gestures as he turned in circles to address her and point toward the sunroom. He seemed like a whole continent reserved for her to explore.

In the sunroom, Peter studied his subject. Pacing, he

glanced between Muffy and her background. He could see by her expression how uncomfortable she was.

He stopped. The air was stuffy. She moved her leg and he could see it stuck to the cushion. Even the light was wrong. The sun was still too high.

"Never mind," he said. His ebullient self ebbed away like air in a slowly deflating balloon. He took her hand and helped her up from the sofa.

"That's really uncomfortable for you, isn't it?"

"The position's fine," she said. "It's just that those wicker arms are so hard."

"And the heat," he said. "We can open the windows. Would a pillow under your shoulder help?"

Muffy glanced back. "I don't think so."

As he strolled back through the house and flipped the thermostat to cool, he struggled to conjure up a suitable site for his model.

Shouldn't have been so cheap. Should have bought a sofa. Didn't plan on guests. Didn't plan on her. Now what?

Muffy followed Peter through the sizzling sunshine up to his studio. He closed his wide, west windows and turned on the air conditioners. One hummed; one clattered. To mask the racket, he started a CD of Mozart's flute concertos.

The music brought Muffy back to the music room. For a moment, she was lying on the sofa again as her mother played. She imagined drifting on clouds. The sound of his voice returned her to the studio.

"How about a picnic?" he asked.

"Sure." She followed him into the kitchen. He took a loaf of seven-grain bread from his cupboard and then vanished into his bedroom. Seconds later, he emerged with a huge, white comforter and a big tackle box.

Muffy took the blanket and folded it into a bulky square. It smelled like a sleepy summer afternoon.

Peter was silent as he tucked a Tupperware box, silverware, and sodas into the tackle box. Then he turned and grinned.

"We'll go to Ridley Creek Park," he said.

Muffy had been there in elementary school to watch people in Colonial costumes demonstrate a life she wanted no part of. But the park was big. There would be beautiful parts she hadn't seen.

She followed him down the stairs, leaving Mozart to entertain the walls. After locking his own door, he swung open the door protecting the Rolls.

Muffy set the blanket on one side of the long backseat while Peter set the picnic box on the floor. They each opened one silver front door. The white leather seats and polished wood of the dashboard were as immaculate as Mrs. Pearlman's house and grounds.

"You know," said Muffy, "I'm really just a boring bean counter in disguise, but if I were the IRS or the SEC or even Alexandra Sergeant, I'd flag your account for an audit, Mr. Gant."

Peter turned the key and pushed a button to fill their spacious compartment with quiet violins.

"Audit away, Ms. Sergeant. My receipts are in the shoebox under my bed." He turned toward her, grinned, and then drove the car onto the drive. After closing the door behind him, he glanced at Muffy.

"If you own a Rolls Royce," she said, "why do you live in the carriage house?"

Peter eased onto the street. "I drive Mrs. Pearlman's car while she's away. I prefer my bike, but cars need to be driven."

"Bike?"

"Ever see a bike stuck in traffic?" he asked. "Nope. Ever feel the wind on your face in a car? Nope."

She thought about the wind on her face on horseback. Wonderful feeling. But since the day James and Suzanne were riding and Suzanne fell, she'd done very little riding outside the ring.

"Do you ride horses?" she asked.

His face hardened. He slowed for a red light. Without looking at her, he said, "When I was seventeen, my friends and I stole a car and hit an Amish buggy. The horse had to be put down."

Shocked silence filled the air between them.

Muffy swallowed. She felt like she had when she saw her father's lab coat after an emergency delivery. Suddenly she knew more than she wanted to.

The light turned green. The tension in his face evaporated. "The good part was, I was chosen from my class of delinquent peers to go to Glen Mills School for Boys."

Muffy forced her mouth to stay shut.

"It was like a prep school. Rows of fraternity houses, great sports, great classes. Run by an ex-gang member from Chicago. Of course everybody watched our every move every minute, but it was better than the orphanage and—"

"Orphanage? I . . . I thought you said you were Cinnsealaigh Steel. And don't orphans go to foster homes? Get adopted?"

"The Cinnsealaighs were brilliant but not always honest and rarely frugal. They squandered the money and most of them died young. My grandmother took me to the home in Warminster before she died, but the papers were never sorted out for adoption."

Muffy sat mesmerized. Was that where she was headed? No. They had money left and her father was alive.

"Did you . . . um . . . further pursue a life of crime?" she asked.

"No."

He looked sincere, but she wasn't sure she believed him. And maddeningly, she found herself intrigued.

"Really?" she asked. "You wouldn't just say that?"

Serious again, he replied. "If I were going to lie, I wouldn't have told you the first truth."

PAFA? Magna cum? Delinquent? Video games? What a mix. Don't get involved. Just eat dinner. Then go home. Watch TV.

He eased into the left-turn lane. "Now you know my deepest secret. What's yours?"

Her face burned and her arms automatically rose to cover her chest.

"Never mind." He turned the car down a narrow road. "Let's start with something easy, like, is Muffy your real name?"

"No. It's Alexandra Madeleine Sergeant. My father, Alexander Sergeant, calls me Alexandra. My mother, Madeleine Marie Maridor Sergeant, called me Maddy's Little Muffin." She raced through her baby name.

"Muffin," he whispered.

She pictured Peter as a little redheaded boy hiding behind a sketch pad and pencil. "When did they die? I mean, do you remember your family?"

"I remember a big house, but not the people in it."

Questions bubbled in her mind behind pensive eyes, wrinkled brow, and closed lips.

Peter followed the road winding through the park and up a hill. He stopped the car by a meadow. The colonial village was nowhere in sight. Instead, acres of wild grasses and flowers climbed to meet the forest home of deer and hawks.

"Do you come here to paint?" she asked as they carried the picnic gear to a level area halfway up the hill.

"I'm more a studio artist than plein-air. I sketch and note colors outside, but I paint inside. Alone."

He opened the boxes and bags of food and began constructing a fantastic sandwich. Cheeses and sprouts, pickles and lettuce, all garnished with beautiful, orange chutney from a tiny jar.

In his hands, the sandwich looked small. On the napkin, it looked huge. Her mind was so full she couldn't ask another question, so she filled her mouth with food. Yummy. He claimed his friend was the chef, but Muffy wondered. Did his creative self overflow into the rest of his life? She wouldn't ask. After his revelations on the way to the park, she couldn't even imagine his answers.

Peter set his Vanilla Coke in the grass and twisted the can

to settle it. Then he reached into the bottom of the tackle box, removed an open magazine, and set it on the blanket at Muffy's crossed legs. In the page of classified ads, one was marked with yellow highlighter.

"Philadelphia Figure Society," she read. "Helen Latimore always submits to them. Never gets accepted. Sublime Recline. Four thousand. Nice prize."

"That's what I want you to pose for," he said.

"Sublime Recline. That means lying down, right?"

"Yeah. The great artists all do figures. Beautiful, like Rubens. The lines of a woman's reclined body are . . . sublime." He shrugged, grinning.

"You mean nude."

"No. I studied figure. In nudes, you see body parts. In the draped figure, you see line and tone, mood. The model's body suggests rather than limits." He snapped his mouth shut. "You know all this."

Her imagination flashed a slide show of paintings from art history classes and The Arts Center exhibits. Sadly, her center's examples of figures fell well short of the mark. She'd only seen Peter's portraits of Leah. What would he do with an entire body? What would he do with her?

"What do you have in mind?" she asked.

"Just you."

His eyes sparkled and his skin glowed in the early evening light. The breeze carried the scent of newly mown grass. Muffy imagined a protective bubble surrounding them in this perfect place. Neither Dr. Sergeant nor Henry Halliday could ruin this moment.

"When you finish your sandwich, could you stretch out, try some of the poses from the sunroom?"

"Sure."

As the sun sank closer to the tree line, Muffy watched the artist concentrate, frown, change his angle of view. She lay on her back and then her side.

"This side is better," he said. "The light is perfect, but I need a focus. A mood. You are more than a beautiful woman. We need a prop. Not a book. Not a mirror. Not a pet."

"A flute," she said. "My mother's. Do you remember asking?"

Chapter Eight

"Yes. Your mouth. So you do play."

"Not really. Not yet. I can only remember one baby song she taught me. But I'm going to find a teacher."

"Show me how you'd hold it," he said.

She held her fingers along an imaginary line to the right of her mouth. Gazing up at him, sunlit gold framed her face.

His mouth spread into a smile she could feel in her bones.

"Where is it?" he asked.

"In my car."

"You really have it with you? Let's go back. The light's going, but I can get it in my place tomorrow. You need a drape. I need a sofa. You really have a flute?"

Muffy set her purse on his card table along with the flute case. While Peter emptied the tackle box, Muffy assembled the instrument. The last of the sun glinted on the keys as she held it to her lips.

"Perfect," Peter whispered. "You're perfect."

She closed her eyes and played the one simple melody she knew.

When she finished, he said, "I love classical music, as you know by now. Are you going to play? Take lessons?"

She struggled to shut out the snarl of bills and statements

itching to explode in her mind. "Soon," she said lowering the flute and twisting the head joint to remove it from the body.

From Muffy's bag, they heard the muffled ring of her cell phone. She sighed.

"Probably Niki, wanting to talk about the garden party," she said. "Or my father, whom I won't allow to ruin this day."

"Or," suggested Peter, "it's a friend who lost my card and needs a portrait."

Muffy rolled her eyes and opened her bag. Checking the caller ID, she confirmed that it was Niki.

"Hi," she said. As she listened to Niki's panicked voice her spirits sank to the floor. "Okay. Thanks. Bye."

She closed the phone and then looked up at Peter. "My father. I can't remember a sweet day he hasn't ruined. Drove himself to Central County Medical, bleeding. A colon something. One of his colleagues called home. Grace is out. Called Niki."

Peter took her hands. "What can I do?"

As her mind went blank, his long arms enveloped her. She basked in his embrace. With her eyes closed, she listened to the low, slow beat of his heart and filled herself with his warmth.

Easing away, she tried to smile, but couldn't do it. As always, her efficient business self took over, put the phone back in her bag and the flute parts back in their case.

Peter watched her gay self surrender to the efficiency of the professional woman. "Do you want me to go with you?"

"No."

He walked her to her car in silence. Before he could catch her chin to kiss her good-bye, she opened the car door, passed him his jacket, and tossed herself and her belongings inside. He wondered if the muse he'd glimpsed would ever return.

Just before she vanished behind the street hedge, she returned his wave. Thunderheads gathered in the southern sky.

Back inside, he retrieved the canvas from its hiding place in the studio corner. That morning, James had come for Leah's portrait and Peter had begun painting from the sketches he'd made after the birthday party. Studying the outlines of Muffy's contented slumber aroused feelings he didn't want to acknowledge.

Leaving the easel, he wandered back into the kitchen and gazed out at the coming storm.

I really don't need a woman in my life right now. Especially not the way you make me feel. I'd be back at AxshunArtz in a heartbeat earning whatever it took to make you smile. Then I'd never be the fine artist I need to be.

But will you even have time for me now?

Thea's red van swung around the drive and parked in front of his door.

June twenty-sixth. Three weeks. No guarantee I'll even see you, Muffy, let alone paint you.

He mentally posed Thea on a scarlet chaise, draped her in gold silk, and placed a whisk, then a pineapple, and then a spice grinder in her hands. The picture was gaudy cartoon art. He could conjure no image as sublime as Muffy playing her golden flute.

Before Muffy left for the hospital, she sorted through the papers on her father's desk in the forbidden den. Recently paid bills and receipts sat in a stack on the stained blotter waiting to be filed. No sign of anything from Halliday. There should have been copies, or faxes.

"Why aren't the transfers here? That was supposed to be done yesterday."

Muffy pressed her questions behind her lips. She wondered when she'd be able to voice them and when she would get a minute to reflect on the turmoil in her life and plan a path forward. Trudging back out to her car, the new concern about her father's health joined the resurfacing money worries.

Fear followed her to the hospital. Giant halogen lights cast an eerie glow over the parking lot. A cluster of employees sat smoking on the bench outside the emergency room. Her father's dark Mercedes waited in the physician's lot closest to the main entrance.

I'll have to get someone to drive that back for me. "I prefer to bike but cars need to be driven . . . stole a car and hit an Amish buggy."

Lightning pierced the sky as Muffy spun through the revolving door. Her heels clicked on the terrazzo floor, echoing in the hospital lobby. After learning his room number from the volunteer at the desk, she tramped down the hall, blind to the old photos of groundbreaking ceremonies for each new addition.

Orphan. Will I soon be an orphan? Would that feel like a curse or a blessing?

In the elevator, she pressed 2 and "Door Close." The rising box was deep enough for a gurney. She wondered if her mother had ridden on a gurney in this elevator. Although the hospital was her father's second home, Muffy had stayed away since her mother's death. When friends came to give birth or receive healing, she sent cards and flowers but waited for their discharge before visiting.

Two dings announced the floor. The doors parted before a nurses' station.

"Room 212?" she asked.

Dark eyes set in a plump face connected the number with the name. "Miss Sergeant."

Muffy nodded.

The nurse hesitated. "He's stable. We're giving him fluids. Colonoscopy on Monday. Doctors are always the worst patients. Maybe he'll be nicer to you."

Muffy found herself in the "holding a yell" pose and then forced a slight smile. "He'll be worse. This way?" She gestured toward the yellow hall.

The nurse nodded. "Good luck."

As she walked along, silently counting off room numbers, she imagined the nurse through Peter's eyes. Would he paint her ample chin or hide it in shadow? Could he use any body under the right drape?

Room 210.

She slowed her pace and paused by room 212. Bracing herself, she strode in. "Good evening," she said to the hulk beneath the sheet. He continued to stare out the window as lightning flashed behind the clouds.

Muffy stood at the foot of the raised bed trying to rouse her party self, trying to remember just one line from years of party conversation. Nothing came. Instead, his snide remarks and orders and all her unspoken retorts battled for her attention.

When her right foot lifted from the floor, she feared she would remove her shoe and fling it at him if nothing happened soon. Instead, she stamped it on the tile floor.

"Hello."

He turned. "Alexandra. How kind of you to drop in."

She had neither sweet smiles nor comforting words to give him, not even faked.

"Did Henry transfer funds?"

"What funds?"

"Did he transfer money from the Everest and Richfield Funds into CDs, bonds, and money markets?"

Dr. Sergeant shrugged and turned back to the window.

"Did he call or fax you yesterday afternoon?"

"No."

"Did you get my fax?"

He faced her with an icy stare. "Children speak with their parents, Alexandra. They don't send faxes."

For the first time in her life, she felt pity for her father. He had always demanded proper behavior, professional appearance, and rational decisions from her. Had he followed his own rules? No.

"I spoke with you before I met with Henry," she said. "I sent the fax copy as leverage to force him to act. I assume he hasn't."

The nurse arriving to check his vital signs gave her an excuse to leave. Muffy said a quiet, formal good-bye and agreed to take his soiled clothing home and bring back proper grooming aides in the morning.

* * *

The gold letters of GladPlatter.com swept around each side of the crimson minivan. After parking it in front of the carriage house, Thea Chan retrieved a foil-covered tray from the back.

"Peter, Peter, pumpkin eater, may I come up?" she called.

"Proceed at your own risk," he answered.

Thea laughed and climbed the steps. "Risk? You have a disaster?"

She joined him in front of the easel. The figure on the canvas rested her sleeping face on delicate fingers; her cheek was hidden beneath a wash of gold.

"I wish I were dreaming her dreams," said Thea.

Peter stepped back. "That's a before shot. Her life's getting messy. How's yours?"

He followed Thea into the kitchen. As she set the tray on the table, he studied her hands. She had the whitest skin and darkest hair he'd ever seen. He wondered for the first time how he'd ever paint her without her skin looking fake. Or should he exaggerate it? Make it appear ghostly, transparent.

Sublime recline. A ghost. Would the white comforter be any kind of contrast or would it make that porcelain skin look muddy?

"Peter?"

He struggled back to the present. "Thea?"

"You like my spring rolls, right?"

"I love your spring rolls."

"Try these."

Thea lifted the foil from her tray. Bite-size, golden rolls snuggled in tight rows. Peter pinched one out. "Cold?"

"Yes. I served them chilled."

He popped the treat into his mouth. *Crunchy. Good. Ginger. Hot. Spicy. Carrots.* "Pineapple?"

"You like? It's sweet instead of savory." She popped one into her own mouth. "They didn't go over very well. I've got this whole tray left. They told me to keep it."

Peter recalled Muffy-the-businesswoman's take on Thea's

food. "I don't think your average Main Liner, even the travelers, are into experimental food," he said.

"I know. I should be an artist like you. Then I could be my adventurous self."

"Nobody would buy it. I went through all that abstract, self-expressionist stuff and you know what people want most? Portraits. They want to look at their favorite picture—themselves. Or their loves."

Peter's heart sank. He was as guilty as anyone, caught only minutes before, painting the woman who threatened to be the love of his life. He turned his attention back to Thea.

"How about some strawberry pie? My bribe. I have a favor to ask."

He handed her the *American Artist*, open to the same highlighted page he'd given Muffy. Thea's lips moved silently and then opened as wide as her eyes.

"You want me?"

Not really, but I may not get my first choice.

"I think so," he answered. "The light's wrong now, but . . ."

He took the pie from the fridge and brought it to the table with plates and forks. Thea sank into a chair, rereading the contest ad. Her chin rested on the mandarin collar of a long, scarlet jacket. Its knotted buttons traced a diagonal line from her throat to her waist.

She could easily have chosen her English mother's conservative ways. Instead, she took her Chinese father's culture to the extreme: red and gold for good luck, Tai Chi instead of aerobics, and an altar for spirits instead of Episcopal Church on Sundays.

"The afternoon light will be perfect here," said Peter. "I'll need a sofa. Some Victorian something. Or a chaise. And drapes." He cut generous slices of the glistening red treat and scooped them onto the plates.

"Should I wear my gold dress?" she asked.

"No. I need a theme. Think, 'Sublime.' What comes to mind?" He lifted his hands and his eyebrows, willing Thea to fill the space left by Muffy's flute with some ethereal object from her life.

He watched her glazed eyes and parted mouth waiting for some idea to burst out. None came.

"Your skin is so white," he said. "We can start there. I was thinking a ghost, spirit.... Maybe blue and white. Sky and ghost. A phantom. Sublime recline on a cloud. No. Cliché. Cartoon."

He huffed. "I'll never be a fine artist if I can't think beyond a game setting."

He looked down at the pie and stabbed a berry. Thea divided her wedge into bites with the side of her fork.

"Chinese people use white and blue for funerals and death. Western people have the funeral, cry, and put flowers in the cemetery. All this is not about spirits.

"Spirits live with Chinese people. We feed them fruit and incense. We tell them our problems, ask them for help. But they're invisible. Not a person under a white sheet like your ghosts."

She slid one pie bite after another into her mouth.

Peter scraped the glaze from the rest of the berries onto the edge of his piecrust. "I can't paint invisible, Thea. But maybe I could hint at a figure, a spirit. Through smoke."

"Joss sticks," said Thea.

"Joss?"

"Incense. I have a brass urn." She held her hands in a ten-inch circle. "I'll change the sand. Nice white. I'll bring a pack of joss sticks. You find some drape. Not blue. Bad luck."

She set her fork on her empty plate. "I have to run."

As thunder rumbled and rain pelted the windows, Muffy sat in her office at The Arts Center. She studied her calendar to see if she could fit modeling time into her schedule. Not tomorrow. Sunday, the cast party followed the last performance of *Major Barbara.*

Out of habit, she imagined a reluctant James at her side. She replaced him with a merry, interested Peter.

Would he come? Would I want him? Yes. He could come early. Check out the old costumes and drapes from old sets. Yes.

Dialing his number, a smile relaxed her face.

"Peter?"

"Muffy! How's your dad?"

"He's getting fluids," she answered, all business. "Colonoscopy on Monday. Are you busy tomorrow night?"

"Night? What's tomorrow? An accountants' ball? You need entertainment?"

He sounded so light. So carefree and happy. How she longed to slip back into the day before the phone call.

"So," he said, "do they know what's wrong?"

"I don't know," she answered. "He doesn't say. I don't ask. Tomorrow's the cast party. They'll finish *Major Barbara.* I need to be there. I'd like you to join me. Come early. You said you need a drape. I have a room full of old costumes and fabrics from sets."

"It's going to cost you," he replied in a deep, theatrical voice.

"Well, since I'm losing all the money I've ever had, I guess I'll have to barter. How much for a date?"

"At five ninety-eight a pound that will be . . . well, I'll round it off to twelve hundred dollars."

She pictured him swinging and grinning from the scale in the produce aisle.

"You're not cheap. How about, let's say, twelve hours of modeling? Would that be enough? Or a solo show at The Arts Center? Your choice."

She waited through a puzzling silence staring at the painting of skipping children tethered to a Maypole with colored ribbons. One of the students had taken the Wyeth painting idea and filled it with her own family's faces. Muffy had bought it for her office.

"No deal," he answered.

"What?"

"No deal. You ask me to choose between strawberry pie and crème brûlée. If I can't have both, I'll have to starve."

Muffy was baffled. "Why can't you have both?"

"You heard it, folks. She will pose for twelve hours and give me a show! What time's the play?"

"That's not fair."

"You're right." He chuckled. "I'll throw in another date."

She had to laugh. "The play's at seven-thirty. Come at five. Grace will make us dinner and we'll still have time to check the costume room."

Silence.

"Peter?"

"Thinking. Ah. Can I meet you at The Center at seven? Check out the drapes after the party?"

Her disappointment shocked her. She forced her mouth into a smile so he would not hear the hurt in her voice. "Sure. Whatever. Seven's fine. I'll be in my office. Do you need directions?"

"Nope. I'm good. See you tomorrow. Oh, love to your Dad."

Muffy returned the dead phone to its cradle. "I am such a fool," she whispered. "Here I think I'm simply modeling and simply asking for a casual escort and the truth is I'm getting attached to this penniless delinquent who only wants my body to suggest sublime.

"Alexandra Sergeant, you are an idiot. You had better shape up or everyone will see that you're really Maddy's stupid, needy, little Muffin."

Chapter Nine

Late afternoon light bathed Thea's body. She was round where Muffy was long. She was soft where Muffy was firm and oddly flat where Muffy was full. Differences so subtle only an artist would have noticed. Peter was no longer comparing figures. Sitting at the card table, his chair facing the tableau, he was completely focused on his subject.

She lay in a long, red silk dress on the one-armed chaise longue he'd bought at an estate auction in Bryn Mawr that morning. The chaise was covered in frayed, flowered chintz. Peter draped it with his stark, white comforter.

The problem was the pose. A flutist could naturally recline. Ghosts rose in smoke. Spirits floated upward. He could arrange Thea's limbs in beautiful lines, but the theme didn't fit. The painting would be beautiful, but it wouldn't win.

Should I even bother? And if it doesn't win, would anyone in the world buy it? The Chans? Maybe. But they'd want to see their daughter's likeness, not a disguised suggestion.

Muffy suggested that her father change into his silk pajamas. "Be comfortable. Maybe you'll feel better."

He glared at her. "They make hospital robes for a reason, Alexandra. Take the pajamas back."

At home, she paced and puttered. Her whole life felt as if

someone had pressed reload. The Arts Center, her father, the money, and Peter all revolved around her without her control. Not a familiar feeling. Not comfortable.

She ate a solitary dinner, then drove to The Center. After helping Niki with the last-minute party arrangements, Muffy strolled from the ballroom. Peter stood in the foyer, dressed in the birthday-party tux. Way overdressed for a play.

Don't you have smart-casual clothes? Why couldn't you come sooner? And how can I be so stupidly glad to see you?

"Your clothes are overkill," she said, "but you're gorgeous."

"I have cutoffs and this. How's your Dad?"

"Cranky. I hope they find a polyp tomorrow and snip it out and send him home. How was your day?"

"Why don't you take your hair down?" he asked. "Are you working?"

"Always." She couldn't imagine not associating this place with work.

"Where's the theater?"

As they walked through the parking lot, he took her hand and stroked her soft skin. Muffy nodded hellos; Peter noted expressions. With programs in hand, they found their fourth-row, center-stage seats. Peter wedged his tall body into the short space. As Muffy waved to friends, Peter paged through the ads to the cast of characters.

He'd let her think he knew the play. Although he'd seen more hours of video animation than anyone should want to, this was his first live performance.

Reading the names, he couldn't decide if Adolphus (Dolly) Cusins or the actor playing the part had the stranger name. Cinnsealaigh was not common, but it had once evoked wealth. Although he disliked the nickname Pete, it sure beat Dolly.

He'd brought sketching tools to capture expressions and costumes. As the lights dimmed and the curtains opened on Lady Britomart and her son Stephen, Peter's hand lay still. The actors were ugly, the costumes pompous, and the lines so stilted he had to concentrate to follow them.

Lady Brit admonished her son to be a man and then scolded his attempts. Peter fought with himself to neither fidget nor shift position. Did Muffy enjoy this?

His thoughts left the performance and settled around the blond mystery at his side. Had his heart raced ahead of his soul to lure him into such a dull evening?

Stage action regained his attention. Two women appeared, one clad in a Salvation Army uniform, the other in the clothes of British wealth.

The first act ended before Peter could determine the play's point.

"It gets better," said Muffy. "Want to stretch?"

"That's a start." He rose and shed his jacket. After draping it over the red velvet seat, his gaze flitted from old, dyed blonds to trim goatees, a sandalwood fan here, an ivory-handled cane there.

Turning back to Muffy, the audience became a blur of rainbow-colored static. Above the hum of conversation, he heard her greetings.

"Evelyn, this is Peter Gant, our new figure teacher. Peter, this is Evelyn Richardson. Board member. Chair of the garden party."

With a serious face, he offered his hand. "And fine arts critic."

Evelyn quickly completed the ritual greeting. "Really? Figure? I thought you were a still life artist, Mr. Gant."

The lights flickered. "I'll see you at the meeting, Muffy." She gave Peter one more scrutinizing look and moved toward her seat.

"You know her?" Muffy asked as she slid into her own.

"I had a show. Tiny flower paintings. Mrs. Pearlman's idea. Your Evelyn gave me a really scathing review. 'Pedestrian,' I think she called it."

The critic was up and running in Peter's mind. Evelyn had reactivated all the doubts he'd appeased by working at AxshunArtz and allowing his pedestrian talent to earn all the money he might ever need. Maybe he really was just a commercial artist; maybe fine art was only a dream.

No. If I can get Muffy to pose, if I can enter her in the contest, I can win.

The lights slowly dimmed.

The second act was even worse than the first. As a recorder of beauty, he found the beggars at the Salvation Army disgusting and ugly. Snobs and bums. How could Muffy enjoy watching this?

He glanced down, hoping to catch a side of her he could reject. She met his gaze and smiled. He longed to sweep her from this boring trap and capture that smile with his brushes and his lips.

"... you must first acquire money enough for a decent life...." Peter heard this line and forgot his cramped legs. Undershaft, the millionaire, captured his curiosity. He listened to the parry between Major Barbara's father and her suitor, Aldophus Cusins.

"... I can only afford to feed her..."

Peter compared Cusins's situation with his own. *I have a ton of money, Dr. Sergeant. But as you must see in your own portfolio, income's down to almost nothing. Not a good time for an emerging artist to court a bride.*

He felt her shoulder press against his own. Warm. Deliberate. What was she doing? Playing with him? Or was he the one playing the date? The fine artist?

"But I feel that I, and nobody else, must marry her," said Cusins.

Although Peter had spent very little of his imagination on his full future, he tried. He couldn't see his elderly self hobbling up the stairs of the carriage house any more than he could see himself enduring more plays. Pictures of painting Muffy pregnant, nursing, and rocking her old body startled him and then felt right.

"I never ask for what I can buy," said Undershaft.

I never buy what I can barter. If I squander my money like an old Cinnsealaigh, I'll have to prostitute my art again.

By the third act, Peter was engaged in the play and its questions of money and morality. Unlike Undershaft, he'd never considered poverty a sin or a crime.

Would I have stolen the car if I had parents to provide one? No.

He focused on the actors. Undershaft needed an aggressive, self-starter foundling for a successor.

I've got the drive and the energy, Dr. Sergeant, but you'll need a doctor to fill your shoes. Are you that sick? Will you need a successor?

At last, the curtain fell on Undershaft's rich, happy life; the lights rose on the complications of Peter's.

Muffy hardly heard the play. She read Evelyn's reviews. The woman saw talent before it emerged. Unfortunately, that was rare. Most of her reviews read more as an exercise to flaunt her wit than to encourage the talent of local artists.

Could she be right about Peter? Muffy had only seen two of his paintings. Was he ordinary? Boring? No. Part of her wanted to snap at Evelyn, defend this new artist. Her sensible self knew she needed Evelyn's cooperation on board matters. This kept sweet smiles and compliments on her lips throughout the cast party.

When the last guests had left, she left the ballroom to Consuela and led Peter through the entrance hall and up the great stairs.

"What direction is this window?" he asked, nodding at the expanse above the seat on the landing.

"West."

A smile lightened his face. "Perfect. Perfect. We could pose you here, after work."

Muffy imagined the sun on her back and Peter's gaze on her face. A comfortable position. "Come," she said, walking toward the stairs to the third floor.

Two long, parallel coatracks filled the stuffy little room. Peter followed Muffy into the narrow space between them. While he pushed crowded costumes apart on one rack, she sorted curtains hung on the other.

As he extracted a purple velvet jacket, a lime satin gown slumped to the floor. He held the fitted, brass-buttoned uniform to Muffy's chest. Not that he wanted Miss Sergeant to look like one, but he wanted to see the effect of cool tones on her skin.

He rescued the green gown and replaced the jacket.

"You, Madam, are a cool-toned woman. Royal violet. You have any cool reds over there?"

Muffy pulled out a rough, wine-colored slipcover.

He shook his head. "No." His long arms wedged the costumes back between their neighbors.

"Let's see what you look like on the window seat," he said.

"There's no light."

"There's enough. I want to get a feel for the place. And see you in it."

Following close behind her, he saw wisps of her golden hair escaping the knot of the bun. He shoved his hands in his pockets to keep from freeing it all.

Let her do that. Don't touch her.

The cool air of the second floor did not cool his desire for his model. Watching her lay on the window seat made it even worse. He backed away and looked around. His video-game mind lifted the cushions and hid the Princess. Lifted the cushions and found the gold. Lifted the cushions, jumped inside, and hugged and kissed the Princess.

Neither of my ideas work. I have beautiful models, great props, and all I can think of are game settings.

He shook his head. "I'll have to sleep on it."

"Before you do that," she said, "could you come with me to the hospital? I need to bring my father's car home."

It was after midnight when she brought the silver tray to the music room. Although live music had not been played here for years, both Sergeants still referred to the place as Madeleine had.

Muffy set the tray beside her laptop on the tiger-maple cof-

Sublime Recline 77

fee table. After pouring her tea into the thistle-patterned cup, she leaned back against her great grandmother's crazy quilt.

The chandelier cast soft light over the flowered wallpaper. How wonderful it would be if her mother were here to share the tea and help her sort through her hopes and fears.

Muffy stretched her bare feet beyond the hem of her long, white gown and gazed past them to the end of the sofa. It was long enough for even Peter Gant, fine artist; Peter Cinnsealaigh, mystery man.

She was surprised when he didn't hold a pencil all evening. She'd felt him stiffen when the lines turned to money and the financial support expected from Undershaft.

At the cast party, she'd asked if he wanted to sketch the actors. He'd declined. "Only you."

Before he left, his sketching hands had held her face under the dark portico. The warm glow he usually kindled in her chest had sucked the air from her lungs and burst into flame. The kiss that followed was neither friendly nor gentle. Only the presence of Grace Gazner kept her from inviting him in.

As his fingers traced her back, she knew he was recording the planes and curves to be drawn later. She didn't care. As she tried to say good-bye, those broad hands drew her closer.

Sipping her tea, she shifted back to the conversations at the party.

"Who's your friend?"

"Peter Gant, fine artist."

"Is he going to teach?"

"Figure class."

"He'd be a great Don Quixote."

"Too busy."

That was the first time she thought of herself as his agent. "Talent is only a part of success, Mr. Gant. If I can manage an entire art center, I can certainly manage one career."

That thought brought her back to the business she was directing. Most of the board had come to the party. Henry Halliday and Evelyn Richardson were as absent as Dr. Sergeant.

The doctor's colonoscopy was set for 9:00 the next morning. Muffy would go in early, wish him well, and spend the next hour on her cell phone.

After returning her cup to its saucer, she opened her laptop, intending to plan the board meeting. She was too tired. As she thought "Program," her fingers typed "Pedestrian."

Is he? Am I really just infatuated with a portrait? Or its painter?

Chapter Ten

Monday arrived cool and clear, a welcome breath of fresh air. So did Mrs. Pearlman. After two weeks in Europe, she was a flustered, sophisticated whirl of enthusiasm and jet lag. Peter sat sipping iced tea in her sunroom while she described fashions and flowers. He saved his own news until Leah arrived.

"I leave for two weeks and each of you simply bolt into happily ever afters!" The plump, old, silver-curled, gold-jeweled woman winked. "And you weren't so easy to find my dears."

"I'll stay until you find a replacement," said Leah. "I haven't even begun to plan the wedding."

"I'm not leaving," said Peter. "It's just a week at the shore and a class at The Arts Center."

"Yes, Peter, you say that now, but I see a look in your eye that wasn't there when I left."

Muffy stood in the waiting room. The surgeon stood in his scrubs. "We only got through the transverse. There's a block."

"Cancer?" asked Muffy.

"Probably. We took a biopsy. Going to keep him. Schedule surgery tomorrow. McCarthy's good, but Alex may want to go to Jefferson in Philly. Ask him. Not now. He's groggy. Wait till this afternoon."

"Me?" she asked.

"I think he'd rather hear it from family than friends."

He'd rather not hear this at all.

The doctor patted her arm, then disappeared into the hall.

Telling her father he had cancer would be hard. Visiting him now and pretending he didn't would be impossible. Muffy stared blindly into the empty hall. From a place in her soul she didn't know existed, tears welled in her eyes and trickled down her cheeks.

Little thoughts of messy mascara, colostomies, and orphans mixed a mud pie in her mind. She didn't move. She didn't yet wipe the tears. The cell phone rang in her briefcase. She ignored it.

Peter listened to a generic voice tell him Ms. Sergeant was not available.

"Yes, Ms. Sergeant. This is Mr. Cinnsealaigh. How's your Dad? Call me when you get a chance. I'm planning the class. See you Wednesday morning."

He paused. Was she listening? "Muffy? Call me, huh?"

Muffy wiped her eyes, picked up the now-silent briefcase, and carried it into the hall. She could go to the lounge. She could go to the cafeteria. Instead, she trudged along the halls to the elevator and pressed 2.

The visitor's chair in Dr. Sergeant's room offered sturdy oak arms and blue vinyl upholstery. Muffy tried to concentrate on special events and fund-raisers for The Arts Center. She'd planned on presenting the program committee with a prioritized list of ideas. When they wheeled her father in, she still only had a folder full of business cards, newspaper clippings, and lists of web sites.

She forced herself to look in his eyes. He knew. She would only have to supply the details. She wouldn't have to pretend. This time when the tears welled, she bent her head and willed them back while she closed her work.

A nurse replaced the IV bag. "Nothing by mouth," she said. "Just ice chips. And just a few."

Muffy nodded and let the woman finish settling him in with comforting murmurs. "If you need anything, just buzz. Dr. Johns will be in later."

When the nurse left, the reclining father stared at the sitting daughter. A gentle smile relaxed his face.

"In a moment, Alexandra, I want you to look in the mirror. Anyone else would disagree, but I've never seen you look lovelier."

Thank you for rescuing me. Thank you for not making me lie. "Dr. Johns said there's a block."

"I know. It's been there for some time."

"How did you know? And why didn't you . . . ?"

"I'm a doctor. I know these things. At the same time, I'm God. I'm immune."

Muffy bit her index finger and rose. She groped her way to the bathroom through a film of tears. Behind the door, she laid the paper towel crease against her lashes and then looked in the mirror. Dark streaks remained beneath her eyes. Even waterproof mascara smudges when you cry and wipe your eyes.

She blew her nose and cleaned her face the best she could. Returning to the foot of his bed, she longed to either have him hug and comfort her or to hug and comfort him. Instead, she clasped her elbows and said, "Dr. McCarthy could operate tomorrow. Or would you rather go to Philly?"

"McCarthy's fine."

"I'll call Mrs. Lind and have her reschedule."

"No."

"But you can't—"

"I know. I don't know if or when I'll be able to. Have her call around and see who's taking new patients."

Muffy dropped her eyes and nodded. The tears were threatening again so she blinked fast and asked, "What did you find lovely about smeared mascara?"

A soft voice replied. "My daughter might, in some remote way, still love her father."

The Haviland family's fine Sheraton-style chairs circled the table and perimeter of the dining room of The Arts Center. Although the room was awkward for viewing an exhibit hung on its walls, the executive committee refused to alter the room or hold its meetings anywhere else.

Muffy arrived at 6:45 in a creamy, fine-knit cotton dress. Her gold hair sat in a tight knot on her head; three aspirins sat in a tight knot in her stomach. She opened her briefcase and set a stack of agendas at the end of the table.

Please let Halliday come. Please let everything turn out. And please let Peter cheer me up when this awful day is over.

The chairs slowly filled with familiar figures. Lee Griffin of Griffin and McClure; Martha Adams, president of First Savings; Judge Brenner of the grand, handlebar mustache; Evelyn Richardson, local columnist and art critic; and Dr. Martin Sinclair, dean of the local business college. By 7:10, two chairs remained empty.

"Good evening," said Muffy. "Thank you for coming. To save your time, I'll cover the monthly business tonight as well as address the financial situation.

"First, my father's fine. Having minor surgery tomorrow. Should be home by the end of the week.

"We'll start with item two and give Mr. Halliday all the time we can."

By 8:30, they had scheduled the play, *Are We There Yet?*, a debut by a local playwright. Big cast comedy. Lots of parts for all ages. Lots of tickets to be sold to family and friends.

They approved a black-tie Christmas reception honoring local, award-winning artists. After a lively debate, they formed a committee to recruit graffiti artists and use their talents to design and paint murals on the town's abandoned buildings.

"Do any of you know where Henry might be?" asked Muffy.

Only glances and shrugs answered her question.

"Do Halliday and Crawford manage any of your accounts?"

The light air of camaraderie evaporated.

So my father is the only idiot to invest with them, or no one else will admit it.

"I believe the endowment may not have been allocated to the most conservative funds."

"Exactly what are you saying, Muffy?" asked Sinclair.

Muffy looked straight through him. "Only Halliday, as treasurer, has full access to the endowment right now, and only Halliday and Crawford have the bank statements. I need your vote to, one, give me authority to access the accounts and, two, demand full and immediate disclosure of where and how the endowment is invested."

The members looked stunned. "Why?" asked Sinclair.

Muffy clasped her papers and found her face reddening. "Mr. Halliday . . . has invested my trust . . . in four front-end-loaded funds which are losing money. To my knowledge, he has not transferred the money to the safer vehicles I requested. He forgot The Arts Center's financials I asked him to bring to our lunch on Friday."

Silence.

Muttered angry words.

"Your father and Halliday are buddies, aren't they?"

Muffy sighed. "My father is a doctor. Not a businessman. I believe he was deceived. And, I suspect The Arts Center has been deceived as well. May I have motions for the authority to explore this?"

She got what she asked for as well as pitying glances and mumbled criticisms. The members agreed to meet in a week.

Once they were all gone and the old house was quiet, Muffy opened her briefcase to return the papers. There was her cell phone. She'd forgotten about the unanswered call in the hospital waiting room. After the tones of the message-retrieving buttons, there was his voice. Warm, delicious, happy, soothing Peter.

She replayed the message and checked her watch—9:15. She played it one more time and then put the phone back with the papers and turned out the light. Locked the door. Climbed into her car and drove away.

What a beautiful voice he had. He'd be wonderful in a play. Wonderful to play with. Snuggle with.

Racing along the Blue Route, she cracked the windows and let the cool summer air fill her senses. She was anxious to see what ideas he'd come up with for the contest. Anxious to let his smile erase all the tensions of her day.

Reaching the right drive in Paoli, the lights were on in the big Victorian house, but Peter's place was dark.

"You idiot!" Muffy chided herself. She parked the car to consider her options.

His landlady must have returned. I should have called.

She checked the car clock, 9:55.

I guess it is late. I didn't think. And that's not like me.

The front door of the big house flew open. Peter burst onto the porch. "Wow! Look who's here."

Long strides brought him to her door in seconds. Although she had intended to return his hug as a simple greeting, her arms hung on. She bit her lip and pressed her forehead into his warm chest. After several deep breaths, she pulled away. "I'm sorry. It's been such a rotten day. I needed a hug."

He smiled. "You're in luck. I've got hundreds right here." He held his arms wide. "And bags more upstairs."

"Oh my," said Mrs. Pearlman, stepping out from behind Peter. "You must be Muffy. Yes, well, I was going to ask you in for biscotti and tea but, are you all right, dear?"

"I'm fine," said Muffy. "No. Not fine. But, I'm better now. You must be Mrs. Pearlman."

"The one but not the only. Pleased to meet you." She offered a hand with pearly polished nails glistening in the porch light. "I just got back this morning. Peter's been helping me fight the jet lag, but I'm finished. You will make an appointment so we can discuss your young man's career, won't you?"

My young man?

Muffy nodded and watched the old woman in her layers of

filmy, flower-printed fabric float back to her house. Returning her gaze to Peter, she saw a tenderness she'd not seen before.

"Want to tell me about your day?" he asked.

"My father has cancer. Surgery tomorrow. Henry Halliday, The Center's treasurer and our own, probably not-so-ethical financial advisor, didn't show."

He frowned. "Sounds like you need a day at the beach. Your friend Heather's picking me up after class on Wednesday. Could you come down on the weekend?"

Muffy shrugged. "If my father's okay."

Peter spread his hands across her shoulders. "Sheepshank of the trapezius, Ms. Sergeant. You need a massage."

For a moment, she stared at him in wonder. "So you studied anatomy in Boy Scouts?"

He turned and guided her toward his door. "I loved anatomy. And I had a class where we drew knots. Learned texture, shadows, and how to follow what's hidden so you get it right when it reappears. Great class."

Taking her hand, he led her up the dark, wooden stairs. One air conditioner hummed, the other rumbled. Neither had succeeded in removing the afternoon's heat.

Peter dropped her hand and switched on the light. A wide amber dish on the ceiling cast the studio in a golden glow.

He led her to the chaise longue.

"So you found the seat," she said, floating down onto the comforter draping the chaise. Peter sat beside her and laid his hands on her shoulders. His thumbs found the square knot and the surgeon's knot as well as the sheepshank. As his accomplished fingers located and untied knots she hadn't known were tied in her back, her mind loosened as well. The walls that separated its compartments swung open.

"My daughter might still love her father," opened memories of love. Playing doctor with Florence, her white Persian kitten. Listening to her heart with her father's stethoscope. Hit by a car. No more pets.

James. Walking ponies in the stream. Preteens. Suzanne's fatal fall from her horse. James's grief. No more shared rides.

"Feeling better?" asked Peter.

"The more you rub, the better it feels, but ₁ think I must have a lifetime of knots stored in my back." *And my heart.*

"And your shoulders." He ran his hands down her arms like he would squeeze water from a wet cloth. "Your arms are fine."

"Is it killing you to just touch and not sketch?" she asked.

"No and yes." He continued tracing her shoulder blades and vertebrae with his fingertips. She flinched when he found tender spots. His fingers lingered, pressing gently. He seemed to sense when Muffy felt a gentle heat replace the pain. He moved on.

She drifted back to her memories of love. All painful. Her mother's, the worst. She remembered turning into a robot. Bringing water and flowers to her dying mother's room. Tuning her father out. Blaming him for his failure.

"Why don't you lie down," suggested Peter. "I can't reach your waist."

They rose. Muffy stretched out on her stomach, arms at her sides. Peter sat beside her, pressing and smoothing her whole back with his palms.

In her mind, people began congregating on the open porch that wrapped around her home. James sat on the railing. Her mother and Vivienne Waite climbed the stairs, arms filled with flowers. Her father came out the door holding Florence.

And there was Peter, taller than all of them, weaving between them, sketchpad and pencil in hand. "Great chin there, Mrs. Sergeant. Can you try to smile, James? Now, Doc, if you're going to be a model, you'll have to loosen up."

As Muffy dreamed, Peter carefully lifted his hands from her shoulders. Nestled in his bedding in the dim light, he could barely see her figure. Not a pose he could use.

He rose and studied her reclined body. Even with a chaise and the best model, the composition and the palette would not come together.

He was tempted to stretch out beside her, join her in sleep, and give her the quiet comfort she so desperately needed. Would she mind? Should he simply go to his own bed and let her sleep here? Or should he wake her and send her off into the dark?

Chapter Eleven

On her drive home, Muffy tried to close the gates in her mind that Peter had opened. She couldn't. It was fortunate that the traffic was so light as memory after memory rose to the surface. She didn't fight the tears. Better to shed them in private than fight them in public.

What was it about this Peter? Whether he was sketching her or rubbing her back, he relaxed her into a dreamy slumber. And the tears. She hadn't cried in years. Was it the seriousness of her father's situation, or was Peter's touch exposing old wounds?

He had woken her with a gentle kiss on the cheek. Given her choices. Looked disappointed when she'd chosen to leave and sad as he closed her car door and watched her drive away.

After a restless night's sleep, she arrived at Central County Medical. Lying on a gurney with an IV dripping antibiotics and relaxation into his waiting body, Dr. Sergeant looked inscrutable.

Muffy reached for his hand. He gripped it and pulled her toward him. She felt the knots in her back retie themselves. He pushed her hand away as the aides entered his room to wheel him to surgery. Muffy followed them down the hall and watched him disappear between swinging steel doors.

Good luck, Father. May it be just a tiny, contained growth.

Sublime Recline 89

Difficult as you are, you're the only father I have. Only parent I have.

Thoughts of Peter as a little boy attached to no one crowded out her present. She imagined the self-reliant Peter she was getting to know. For a moment, she basked in his comforting embrace.

No. You don't even know him. Get to work.

The hard walls and floor magnified the sound of her steps as she trudged to the surgical lounge.

As Muffy waited, Peter packed.

Standing before the little closet, he took T-shirts and shorts from their hangers and folded them into an old leather satchel. He added underwear and his Gant shirt and then set it on the floor.

What if he hadn't woken her? Would she have slept through the night? Could he have forced himself to leave her on the chaise and sleep alone in his bed?

"You will never know, Peter, ole boy. Perhaps, if she comes to the shore, you'll uncover another layer of the mystery woman."

From under his bed, he retrieved the tackle box. Inside, he kept small sketch pads, a few sharp pencils, and a kneaded eraser.

Three shelves of the bookcase at the head of his bed were filled with sketch pads of all sizes. He had saved drawings of everything from dandelion blossoms to the nostrils of horses, babies in strollers, and broken eggshells.

One shelf held art books: Dali, Chardin, Wyeth, Renoir. The last shelf held plaster casts: hands, feet, ears, and one small bust.

Peter took the Chardin, his favorite master of texture and composition, and tucked it into the box. He added two small sketch books taken at random. After wrapping the hands in a souvenir T-shirt from Athens, Georgia, he fit them on top of the book. Teaching aides for his class.

* * *

While Peter packed, Muffy occupied a corner of the waiting room with her briefcase open on a table of tattered magazines. A woman with champagne-colored hair and a volunteer's jacket smiled down at her. "Can I get you some coffee?"

Muffy nodded. That kindness gave her the energy she needed to call Halliday and Crawford.

"This is Alexandra Sergeant. I need to speak with Henry Halliday."

The volunteer smiled and set the Styrofoam cup, sugar, and creamer on the table by the old *Family Circle*. Muffy smiled a thank-you.

"Morning, Muffy. Sorry I couldn't make it to your meeting last night. Got tied up with clients."

"Did you complete the fund transfers I requested, Henry?"

"We're working on it. Any new business?"

"You'll receive the minutes. Since our treasurer is too busy, the board authorized me to review its accounts."

"Muffy, Muffy, Muffy." He chuckled.

It crossed her mind that his insults had no effect on her emotions. Henry Halliday was, at best, a condescending man, at worst, a crook. He didn't scare her or touch her vulnerable heart in any way.

"Our attorney will contact you today, Mr. Halliday. Maybe he can help you hurry those transactions." She snapped the phone shut.

Grateful that her business self seemed to be in control now, Muffy spent the hours of her father's surgery making calls and conferring with Niki. At odd moments, pictures of walking barefoot through Streker's beach house popped into her head, and Peter popped in beside them.

When she saw Dr. McCarthy's green scrubs stop in front of her, she felt internal switches turn her composed self to her emotional self. She rose and pressed her nails into her palms.

"Fortunately, he doesn't have a colostomy," reported the doctor. "Unfortunately, it got a head start on us. I got all I could see, but it's probably spread. He'll need chemo. And then we'll watch him. You'll need to say a lot of prayers. It wouldn't hurt to help him get his things in order. Do you have any questions?"

"How long does he have?"

McCarthy shrugged and shook his head. "I can't tell you. I've seen it all. Could be three months or twenty years. I can't tell you what makes the difference. Sometimes I think it's attitude, sometimes metabolism, but I have no proof either way."

He laid his hand on her knotted shoulder. "Either way, find a way to mend any broken fences. Spend time with him. He needs you. Friends are great, but in times like this, no one beats family."

He checked the clock. "Gotta go. I've got one more today. If there's anything I can do, let me know."

Muffy nodded, watched the surgeon leave, and then packed up her traveling office. She spent the afternoon in slow motion, accomplishing nothing, not even comforting her uncomfortable, semi-conscious father. Finally, she left.

At home, she entered the hall by the dining room and heard Grace Gazner grumbling in the kitchen. The thought of sharing her home alone with grouchy, gossiping Grace made her cringe.

"Oh, Muffy, I thought you'd call after the surgery. How'd our dear doctor do?"

"Just fine, Grace. Is dinner at six?"

"Whenever you'd like it."

It was nearly 9:00 on Wednesday morning when Peter shut the door on the bright red Corvette.

"You owe me one," said Chris, his friend and former partner.

Peter laughed. "Wrong. You're the one paying me back. See ya."

Minutes later, he stood in what had been the master bedroom of the Haviland's house. With lots of northern light, it was the perfect art room.

He paced around a table he had draped in dark velvet to

display the white plaster hands. His students straggled in and began setting their papers, pencils, canvases, and paints on the easels surrounding the table.

Peter moved to the center. "My name is Peter Gant," he said in a voice so quiet they had to hush to hear him. "To make good art you must see. We'll start with hands. I want you to pick one you like and study it. Look for geometric shapes. The whole. The parts.

"Look for values. The lightest lights. The darkest darks. Look for proportions. How wide is the thumb compared to the palm?"

"Where's the model?" asked the one young man.

Peter turned to face the boy. A young artist wanna-be. Peter, himself, a decade earlier. He recalled his own impatience with Northrop Kingston, his teacher, mentor, and nemesis at PAFA.

"Change in plans," said Peter.

Turning to the class at large, he continued, "Study the hand for thirty minutes. It'll kill you. You will be so sick of it you will want to pack up and go home. Stay with it. You'll hit a plateau, and then you'll begin to see. Then, you can begin to draw."

He could already see their agitation—lowered eyes, fidgeting with materials.

"If you want to make art, not just a picture to stick on the wall in the guest room, study the hand."

Muffy sat in her office longing to study Peter's face and hear his voice. Instead, she listened to the head of the potters' guild.

"Whoever you hire to be the caretaker can live here. That room upstairs is too small for us. And the water is all the way down the hall. The gardener's house is perfect.

"We can have more students per class. Make more money for The Center."

Muffy already agreed. Better to have lights on at the Center than hidden behind it. Better to have the kiln out of the house too. "Good idea, Marge. I'll get board approval next week. Can you find some strong bodies to move the equipment?"

Sublime Recline

"Sure. And we'll have room for more wheels and benches."

"Not yet. That's an expense not in the budget. But, get some estimates and we'll figure something out. Does the guild have any money?"

Marge hardened. "That's our money."

"Of course," said Muffy. "Talk to your members. I'm sure you can plan a fund-raiser."

Muffy glanced at her watch and then back to the potter. "See me next Tuesday and I'll let you know what the board says."

Following the woman from her office, she turned and then dashed up the stairs to the figure class. Peeking in the open door, she felt eyes turn from their work to her.

"If you are drawing," Peter said, "and your model moves, you may get lost. The distance from the chin to the neck will be wrong. The profile you were sketching now includes the other eyebrow. What do you do? Do you know enough anatomy and perspective to fix it?"

The students' eyes were back on Peter, back on the plaster hands. They looked like bullied children, wanting to leave but afraid to move.

He hadn't seen her. He must have known someone stood at the door. He must have known it was her, but he didn't acknowledge her.

She turned and quietly retreated down the hall and stairs.

He told me he didn't want to teach. That was one of the first things he said. Now he's only doing it to get me to pose for him. And look at the students. Just standing there listening to him. I love his voice. I'd listen to anything he said. Will they?

When Muffy returned to her office, Niki had ads for the stage manager and cast for *Are We There Yet?* ready for her approval.

"I think I really messed up," Muffy confided. "Peter's lecturing and everyone's just standing there. They came to paint and draw."

"No one's left the class," said Niki.

"No. They'll come here for a refund on their way out."

"You had a call from your dad and your lawyer. Here's the slides of the submissions for the September show."

Muffy nodded as her brain switched into overload. How she would love to be upstairs studying Peter's anatomy. Could she sketch him? Probably not. That was why she was in the office. She loved the art that others made. Loved sharing it. Promoting it.

She called the attorney.

"He's in court," said the secretary, "but he left a message. Halliday and Crawford say there's some confusion about who has the certificates for the funds. Will you be speaking with your father?"

I guess I'll have to. "Thank you Linda. I'll check it out and get back to you."

Next she called her father.

"Yes," a tired voice answered.

"Good morning, Father. Are you feeling better today?"

"No. When are you coming?"

"I have a few things to wrap up here and then I'll be over. Do you need anything?"

Long silence.

"Father?"

"Nothing you could bring."

Now it was Muffy's turn for quiet. What could she say? "Cheer up. You'll feel better in no time." No. She knew his response to false optimism.

"Okay," she continued. "I'll see you soon. Bye."

Niki returned. "The adjustor's here about the tree damage last week."

"Give him phone numbers for Mrs. Burton and Mrs. Latimore. I have to go to the bank and the hospital. I'll see you this afternoon."

She found the father she'd feared for close to thirty years lying unshaven in a heap of hospital linens. Tubes snaked around the sheets carrying fluids in and out. One tube dropped and ran along the floor before it swooped back up to the bag at the foot of the bed.

"Can I bring you anything?" Muffy asked.

"What would that be?" He sighed. "I can't eat. I can barely move."

"A journal? Crossword? Newspaper?"

"For what? My mind?" He turned his eyes to the window.

"Father, did Henry give you the certificates for those funds he bought?"

Dr. Sergeant winced as he tried to raise his legs. "There's a file in my desk. Is Charlie seeing my patients?"

"Mrs. Lind is taking care of everything."

She recalled Dr. McCarthy telling her to mend fences, get things in order. *Not today.*

It was hard to make conversation with a man so miserable. Somehow, she knew Peter could have. She wished he were there. Making jokes. Making sketches. Making the afternoon bearable.

"I have a new teacher at The Arts Center," she said. "Peter Gant."

"Never heard of him."

"You will. He's excellent. Does portraits. He's doing the Strekers. Four generations."

She had snared his attention.

"I wanted . . . I had always thought I'd have more children. But I thought at least you and James. . . . A grandchild would have been nice."

Who is this man? I was supposed to be the businesswoman, not the mother.

"I always thought my career was the most important thing to you," she said.

He sighed and closed his eyes. "Yes, that and giving me grandchildren."

Muffy stood and watched his jaw slacken. Tears stung her eyes and the invisible hand in her chest squeezed her heart.

If I ever have children now, will you live to see them?

She heard the first notes of his symphony of snores. As she turned to leave, a nurse bustled in.

"Is that tube supposed to be dragging on the floor?" asked Muffy.

"No," the nurse answered. "Dr. Sergeant, time to get your temp."

Chapter Twelve

While Muffy set up on-line access to The Arts Center bank accounts, Peter rode down Route 1 toward the Delaware shore.

While Muffy ate Mrs. Gazner's salad plate alone in the dining room, Peter studied the Strekers' eye shapes, cheek colors, and hair textures over grilled pork tenderloins on the screened porch.

While Muffy pulled file after secret file from her father's desk, Peter pushed his feet in the sand and imagined Muffy reclining on the dunes.

By Saturday morning, Dr. Sergeant allowed Muffy to wrap his dark, silk robe over the hospital gown and tubing. At her side, he shuffled to the empty patients' lounge using the IV pole for balance.

He led her to an empty love seat facing a lifeless aquarium. Florescent light illuminated a world of green plastic plants anchored in a bed of algae-covered pebbles. The water was still.

He scowled at the tube connecting the hanging bag to his wrist. "I could use a steak," he mumbled.

"You must feel starved," said Muffy. "At least it won't be long, now. Grace is already planning your favorites."

Settling next to him, she first tried to show him the slides for the autumn show. No interest. She relayed the well wishes from Mrs. Lind, the board members, and friends who'd called. His moods swung from cranky to despondent.

Muffy turned to the window. Leaves of the oaks planted too close to the building hung wilting in the hot sun.

"I'm going to run down to Streker's cottage," she said. "I'll be back tomorrow, probably late morning. How about some saltwater taffy for when you can eat?"

He didn't seem to hear her. "They need to get this thing down. I shouldn't have a temp."

"What is it?" she asked.

"Ninety-nine point eight."

"Father, that's not high. And I'm sure you're the best-watched patient here."

He looked at her as if he were memorizing her face. "You know Alexandra, I only wanted to protect you."

Muffy's face burned and she held her breath.

"You've acted as if I were out of line, but all I did was tell you, as I've told my patients, how to check. I know I've been a fanatic, reminding you so often. But I couldn't bear to lose you too."

Muffy's arms rose as he leaned toward her. She laid her head between his rough cheek and his soft robe. All the hugs she'd held for years slipped through her arms. He patted her shoulders as if he were afraid he'd break her, as if he'd never done it before, as if he were holding back a desperate, crushing hug.

She drew back, smiling, and wiped her eyes. "I'll see you tomorrow." She kissed him on his cheek for the first time in years.

Weaving through the shore traffic, Muffy ran a mental slide show studying pictures of her father she'd recorded since her mother died. He had never touched her. Why had she felt so exposed and vulnerable? Was it being a pubescent girl forced to discuss breasts with a man? Was it associating this man with the source of her mother's illness and death?

She shook her head to clear it. Poor Alexander. Poor Madeleine. Poor little Muffy.

What other assumptions had she made about the man who'd raised her? She found memories springing to view in need of revision. Had he chosen all her clothes? No. She'd shopped at Renée Fortier's alone. But she'd only purchased what she knew he'd approve. And had he been wrong? No. Boring, but not wrong.

"Wrong dress, but you're gorgeous." Peter's first words echoed in her mind. "Not wrong for work, Father, but wrong for a party."

She thought about Dr. McCarthy's direction to mend fences. They'd mended the biggest.

Streker's cottage had no fences, only old broken privets surrounding the low square of gray, weathered shingles. A screened porch wrapped around all four sides of the house. For as long as Muffy could remember, there had been precious summer weeks of falling asleep on those porches, hearing nothing but the ocean.

Inside, the great room was so vast that tables for games and dining, clusters of wicker, and bookshelves for reading still didn't crowd it.

Opening the screen door, she heard nothing.

"Hello," she called and then stepped through the open slider into the great room. In the back corner on the ocean side, the furniture had been cleared away for the easel.

Muffy strolled through the room of memories and stood before the portrait. Four Strekers. Studying their faces, Muffy compared the features. Although their noses, chins, cheeks, and hair were individual, their eyes were identical.

Would my child have my blue eyes? Or would my father's hazel reappear? It had been years since she had pictured the children she assumed she'd have with James. Of course the only way she would ever appear in a four-generation portrait now, would be as the great grandmother.

"You're here!" Peter burst from the seaside porch. His green eyes twinkled.

Muffy felt the commotion in her heart. "Yes."

"How's your dad?"

She shrugged. "He's up. Walking around. Not quite as irritable, but really concerned about a ninety-nine-degree temperature. Your work's going well."

She listened as he described the Streker women's fashion show of portrait clothes. None worked. Fortunately, they had found the perfect combination of blues in Rehoboth's boutiques.

"I put them all on you, in my mind's eye," he said. "And you looked great. If I'd had five hundred dollars, it would all be gone."

Muffy tried to smile and failed.

"So you want to choose your own clothes and break out of that beige uniform by yourself?"

He had misread the reason behind her frown. *I'm sure you would choose prettier clothes for me than either my father or I have, Peter, but at least we could afford them. Will I be able to now?*

"You need a hug?" he asked, interrupting her thoughts.

Without replying, she sank into his arms. She wouldn't think about his poverty or the character flaws behind it. This moment, she savored his warmth, his humor, and the fresh, salt-air smell of his T-shirt.

Hearing the door, she forced herself from Peter's embrace.

"Muffy!" cried Heather, leading the family into the cottage. A sleeping Becca lay over her father's shoulder. "We tried to get Peter to come sailing, but he claimed he had to work."

Before collecting hugs and hellos, Muffy turned a skeptical gaze on the artist. He was not at the easel when she arrived. In answer to the question in her eyes, he smiled wide. Dimples appeared in each cheek. "Cleansing my visual palate."

"Wow, is it hot," said Heather. "Even with the breeze, it's boiling out there. We'll stay in and watch videos this afternoon. When Peter's finished with us." She cast a mischievous grin his way. "Can you work without Becca for a while?"

The afternoon passed with ham and Swiss sandwiches, melon ball compote, brownies, and lots of iced tea.

In the corner next to the wide-screen TV sat an antique cradle filled with Barbie dolls. Muffy thought about the rare rainy afternoons when she and Heather had dressed those dolls for every event they could imagine. They hadn't imagined board meetings and hospital visits, only parties, dances, dinners, and shopping.

She turned and studied Peter. As he mixed and applied dabs of color to the canvas, he was oblivious to everything but his work.

How can he be so talented, work so efficiently, and still have nothing to show for his life at thirty? He must have made some money in video games.

And what do you have at thirty, Maddy's Muffin, that your father hasn't given you?

Muffy felt her face flush and the knots in her shoulders pull tighter.

Over the fireplace, the little bird sprang from the clock to cuckoo five times. Muffy turned and watched Peter drop his pallet into the shallow plastic box. He winked and pointed toward the ocean-side door.

"Excuse me," she murmured, but realized that Heather was dozing. Passing the table where his brushes lay drying, she glanced at the portrait. He had added nothing she could define. It simply looked as though he had turned a focus knob.

"Come," he whispered, taking her hand.

Muffy matched his long strides between the hedges and the storm fences to the dunes. Her bare feet burned on the hot sand.

"You must burn easily," she said.

"Works out great," he answered. "The daylight's too precious to waste outside and the night air's too sweet to waste inside."

Muffy stopped. "You're always so happy. You act like everything is a stroke of good luck. Hasn't anything bad ever happened to you?"

She saw the shadow fall over his face and immediately regretted her words. Before she could apologize, he placed a tender kiss on her lips.

"Yes," he replied. "As long as you have anything left to lose, horrible things can happen. Having nothing of value, wanting nothing material, is pure freedom."

He started to say something else but stopped, took her hand, and returned to a pace as brisk as the soft sand would allow. He walked in silence for several minutes and then stopped.

"Let's try this," he said. "Lie here like you did in the park and pretend that you're playing your flute."

Muffy lowered herself to the sand and wriggled until it conformed to her body. She slung one ankle over the other knee.

Peter frowned.

She bent one leg and stretched the other.

He nodded and pulled a miniature sketchbook from his pocket. The pencil seemed imbedded in his fingers. His face went blank and she could tell he only saw the lines of her bones and the shadows on her flesh.

As warm and tender and fun as he can be, this will never work. How can he like having nothing? How can he think that's freedom? Freedom is having everything you want and not having to worry about how to pay for it.

Her thoughts turned to her own situation. She'd always had everything she wanted. Would she get the money mess straightened out so she could continue?

I will. But if he doesn't want anything, will he have the drive for success? Without that, the best promoter in the world can't help him. I will not get attached to a struggling artist. And I will not wait for his success. I waited for one man. I will not wait for another.

She looked into the sky. A small plane flew just offshore tugging a banner: *Shelly! Marry Me?*

Despite all the rational reasons not to, Muffy mentally replaced the Shelly with Peter. He didn't see the banner; didn't guess at her thoughts. Instead he paced, wrinkled his brow, and then whipped off his T-shirt. After wadding it into a ball, he set it on the sand and directed her to use it as a pillow for her head.

Light bronze hair covered his chest. His shoulders looked more powerful than his gentle hugs had felt. Why couldn't he at least be ugly?

"How did your class go?" she asked.

"They hated it."

No one could hate you. Much as I'd like to, I can't.

"Did anyone leave?" she asked.

"No."

"Then how can you say they hated it?"

"No joy. No 'ah ha!' No art."

Despite her attempt to distract him, the artist remained in control of Peter's attention. Despite her rationalization that there was no future for the relationship, her problem-solving mind searched for access to the man behind the artist's eyes.

She thought about that man. He seemed genuinely interested in her father's health. He seemed able to read her mind and then blurt out whatever he thought she was thinking or feeling. Not hurtful, just blunt. Maybe that was the key.

"So," she said, "you never wanted children?"

His hand froze. Serious eyes met hers.

"Key word there is want," he said. "Until June sixth, all I wanted was to create fine art."

June sixth. James Waite's birthday.

A kaleidoscope of images spun through her mind. *Was it something at the party or something before he came? Couldn't be that old house. Was it access to people who could afford his talent?*

Muffy shrugged, "Something at the party?"

Peter slapped the pad shut and slid it into his pocket.

"Yes." He pulled her to her feet. "You. I can live with nothing. Can you? Can I be happy painting a studio model? Or Thea? No. All I can see is you. Do I want children? Yes. But not unless I can give them all that I missed."

Muffy felt stones piling in her heart. She shook out his shirt and handed it to him. Her questions seemed to open the doors to the same vulnerable spots that his touch opened in her. Instead of enjoying the merry man she'd met last week, she seemed to be drawing out a serious soul. Not what she wanted. Not what she needed right now.

He shook the sand from the shirt and slipped it over his head. As the hot breeze spun shore grasses, leaving circles in the sand, they returned to the house in silence.

The dinner table was set with bright picnic wear. Heather handed Peter and Muffy huge goblets filled with fresh strawberry margaritas. A party. Just like Barbie would have attended. Witty conversation with one fishy pun following another. "Oh clam up." "No way, shrimp." "You can't muscle me out." "I was only floundering around."

Peter's laugh would build behind his closed mouth, then burst out and double him over. No need to even hear the joke; the sound of his laugher was contagious. You had no control—you had to laugh with him.

Long after the minty taste of toothpaste had replaced the flavor of lemon sorbet, Muffy lay wide awake in the daybed on the north porch. Although the linens were new and clean, they immediately absorbed the moist shore air and felt as hot and sweaty as she did.

Nana Streker's puffy little snores filled the silence between each breaking wave. Peter slept on the south porch. *When* he slept. Muffy had seen his tall shadow disappear between the hedges. She controlled the temptation to follow him, but failed to push him from her mind.

Peter pushed his way through the loose sand of the dunes. Without Muffy, his new life would be fine. Everything Mrs. Pearlman had been saying these last months was rushing back to him. Commissions, exposure. A contest win would establish him in the Philadelphia art community.

He hadn't cared about the money. He'd already met that challenge at AxshunArtz. It was the recognition he wanted.

Sublime Recline 105

Recognition would give him the permission he needed to devote his entire soul to his art.

The commission from this portrait and Leah's was fair, but nothing compared to his commercial income, and even less compared with the profit they'd made selling the company. But with the current bear market he had scant interest and dividends to fritter away. The principal would need to last him the rest of his life. At least the life he had dreamed of.

Walking out to the hard sand, he let the waves break over his ankles. He searched the dark sea for inspiration for the portrait background. None came. Only pictures of Muffy's face crinkled in laughter. Muffy's long legs lying on the sand.

Muffy rearranged her long legs once more on the damp sheets. Had he returned? Had she dozed? Would she ever be able to sleep?

Why had he frowned while he sketched her? As the days passed, he seemed no closer to his contest composition.

Maybe he just needs the right drape. Maybe we should go to a fabric store. Maybe a sari.

As she imagined winding yards of gauze around her body, her mind wound into the depths of dreams.

When she awoke, the sky was gray-pink. The sun still hid beneath the horizon. She lay still for a moment, listening for others awake in the house. The only sounds she heard were birds.

She leaned over the daybed and pulled her bathing suit from her carry-on. Under the sheet, she slipped off her nightgown and squirmed into her suit. As quietly as the creaking bed and floorboards allowed, she crept to the screen door, lifted the latch, and stepped out into the dawn.

Soon enough, she would drive back to her own mess of a life. For this private hour she would swim in the empty ocean.

She threaded the storm fences and ran quickly over the sand. On the beach toward town, there were already a few early treasure hunters. A man pushed a metal detector and a couple collected shells.

Muffy dashed across the sand and into the water. She ran until the waves covered her thighs and then dove in. Emerging beyond the breakers, she floated. The cold water was a refreshing gift from the suffocating heat of the last day and night.

She watched the sun sneak over the horizon and then turned her gaze to the empty sky.

"Red sun in the good morning!" he called.

She gasped. "I didn't see you. Did you spend the night here?"

"Not all of it."

They let the water jostle their bodies five feet apart.

"I was thinking," she said. "Maybe we could go to a fabric store. Or an Asian boutique. What about a sari?"

He grinned. "Good ideas. I'm coming back tomorrow afternoon, but you'll be working."

"And I have an executive committee meeting at night."

She shook her head and sank in the trough of a wave. "And then there's my father."

The next wave brought her within his reach. In over her head, she couldn't hold her ground. Peter reached for her hands and drew her close. She didn't resist, simply wrapped her arms around his neck and let her legs tangle with his.

The water jostled them, forcing them closer. His cheeks were rough copper; his eyes liquid green. Her critical, rational mind was somewhere in her suitcase.

Hugging, caressing, they drifted toward shore. When Peter could touch bottom, he stood and held a floating Muffy by her waist.

"You feel as good as you look," he said.

Chapter Thirteen

Doctor Alexander Sergeant was giddy. "I need my multicolored maternity slippers, Alexandra. They're in the bottom drawer."

His last temperature was over 104 degrees.

"He's got Tylenol. It's coming down," snapped the woman wearing a multicolored, fireworks-printed uniform.

With the casual hospital dress code, Muffy couldn't tell whether she was a cleaning woman or the head nurse.

"I need to speak with Dr. McCarthy," said Muffy. "Is he on call or do you have his pager?"

"It's Sunday, Miss Sergeant. You don't want to call him. We've got things under control."

"Code blue, two twenty-six. Code blue," the intercom blared. Staff exploded from everywhere into the hall and ran to the emergency. Muffy turned back to her father.

"The cat's going to keep me company," he said. "It's a Cheshire cat. See him smile?"

Muffy nodded. Here he was, delirious, and all the nurses were saving someone else. She thought about giving him ice water and then wondered if he was still on ice chips.

She had to talk to Dr. McCarthy. She couldn't leave her father. Grace had the day off. Couldn't ask her to call. Niki. She called and got her machine. James.

Reluctantly, she dialed the familiar number for Waitehaven.

As she listened to the ringing phone, she compared sweet Glenna Roberts, the Waite's housekeeper, to her own grouchy Grace. Grace Gazner had hovered and chided and tried to assume the role of Muffy's mother. Now Muffy could see how her little-girl self had resisted and grown to treat everyone with an arrogant indifference. She cringed.

Mrs. Roberts answered. "Glenna, my father's bad. Could you look up Dr. McCarthy's number for me?"

"Why sure, Muffy, hang on."

She waited only moments for the number. As she wrote, her father babbled about red yarn for sutures.

"Thank you, Glenna. Bye, now."

When Muffy left the hospital late that evening, Dr. Sergeant was sleeping, his body dosed with antibiotics fighting the infection Dr. McCarthy had feared.

At home, she made herself a cup of chamomile tea and brought it to her father's desk. Searching for the fund certificates, she had found files of paid utility bills and files of her own tuition bills and grades.

In a folder tucked way in the back, she found pink linen envelopes addressed in her mother's hand. Muffy stared at the script she hadn't seen in years. Graceful cursive lines broke for the tiny capital e. Loops instead of slashes crossed Sergeant's final t. Here was the hand of the woman who loved the man now dying.

Muffy opened the top envelope and unfolded the pink paper. She could hear her mother's voice as she comforted Alex about the death of a patient.

"Poor Father. You've had no one to love you for so long."

She'd forgotten all about the will, advance directives, and the certificates when the phone rang.

"Hello?"

"May I please speak with Muffy?" asked a shaky female voice.

"Who's calling?"

"This is Elane Pearlman. Peter's my caretaker." She sighed. "Is this Muffy?"

"Yes. Is something wrong?"

"Oh, dear, yes. There's been an awful fire. I thank God he wasn't there."

"Where?"

"The carriage house. Burned to the ground. They say electrical. That old air conditioner. I should have replaced it. Then all the lawn equipment. Gas cans."

Muffy pictured Peter's life in flames. Explosions sending the easel, the microwave, and the comforter flying to the treetops.

"I called Leah, but she only knew he went to the shore. Do you know where?"

"When did this happen?" asked Muffy.

"Early evening. My neighbor saw it and called the fire department."

Muffy felt like falcons were landing on her shoulders, their talons sinking into her neck. "Is there anything left?" she asked.

"No. It was frame and shakes. A lot of old wood. I'll rebuild it as soon as I can. I have plenty of room for him here. I'll replace everything he lost, but. . . ."

Did he have any paintings there? You can't replace them. His art has to matter. Doesn't it? Will he still think having nothing is so freeing?

"He's painting at my friend's cottage," she finally answered. "He was planning to return tomorrow afternoon. If you want, I'll call him. Have him come to The Arts Center first and tell him there."

Mrs. Pearlman was silent for a long moment.

"Thank you," she said.

Muffy brought her tea to the microwave and rewarmed it while she collected her thoughts. As much as she would love to end this day with the sound of his voice, she decided to wait until morning. She wasn't sure she could keep her voice light enough to hide the tragedy.

Strolling through the empty house, she wondered how she'd feel coming back to burned rubble.

What would I miss? Photographs. Books. I could replace the books.

The flute.

In a daze, Muffy wandered in and out of the second-floor bedrooms. The guest room with the closet where the luggage was stored had two long windows. Behind the brocade drapes hung creamy sheer curtains. She pulled a wing chair to the window, slid off her shoes, and climbed up to reach the rod.

Back in her own room, she removed her shirt and slacks and tried to wrap the dusty drape around her.

She didn't know how. The curtain certainly didn't flow like those draping the figures of Botticelli's *Venus and Mars*. Peter would know how to wrap it.

She let the curtain drop to the floor and sank to her bed. For a moment, she let the dust of the day settle over her. She pictured climbing into her little red BMW and letting Peter drive her out of their messy lives and into the setting sun.

"No. We're partiers, not escapists. The Arts Center needs a resident. Juan and Consuela will continue with maintenance. The board will simply have to approve Peter."

Muffy readied herself for bed and then found and assembled the gold flute. She hesitated, remembering Mrs. Gazner in her room downstairs.

"Maybe you need a song to soften your heart, Grace."

Standing in the hall at the top of the stairs, she played single notes. The surfaces of wood, carpet, and wallpaper filling the large, open space gave the music a rich sound. She stood, allowing her fingers to choose the notes of her heart's own song. A song never to be written, never repeated, and never performed for an audience.

When it ended, she retrieved her teacup and brought it to the kitchen. No sign of the housekeeper. Checking locks and turning out lights she found herself in the music room.

She lay on the long, blue sofa, holding the flute in the pose he'd sketched at the beach. She filled the room with long, quiet notes, wishing she were a genie who could will him to her presence with a seductive song.

What would he do now? Move in with Mrs. Pearlman? Or could she find space at The Arts Center?

What about me? Will my father die this week? Will all the money be lost? Will the board replace me?

She set the flute on the carpet and pulled the crazy quilt over her legs.

Muffy paused in the kitchen before leaving for work.

"Grace, I'll have a guest for dinner tonight. Peter. He's an artist. New teacher at The Arts Center."

Grace Gazner's shoulders drooped. "So what do you want?"

"I don't know."

I don't even know what he likes. I don't know anything about the inside of him. Only his work and how warm he makes me feel.

"Muffy?"

"Yes. Sorry. Anything. Whatever's easy for you."

As she hurried down the walk to her father's office, she ran a mental video of life without Grace.

Would Mrs. Roberts have been so critical and pushy and sullen? No. Mrs. Roberts was the comfort at Waitehaven. Not James.

After his beloved Suzanne's riding accident, Muffy had been a convenient social partner. She, like everyone else, had simply assumed she always would be.

Until Leah.

"Thank you, Leah," she whispered once more.

Muffy opened the office door and heard the phone ring. As she approached the desk, Mrs. Lind gave her a weary smile. "Dr. Sergeant's office, could you hold please?" She pressed the button to switch lines.

"Thank you for holding. No. He's recovering from surgery. Dr. Welsh is covering. May I give you his number? We're not sure."

Mrs. Lind hung up. "When will he be back?"

Muffy sank into the counter separating the waiting room from the desk.

"Yesterday, he was delirious," she said. "Temperature over a hundred and four. Have you heard of any new docs, grads looking to affiliate?"

Mrs. Lind seemed to wilt. "That bad?" she asked.

Muffy nodded.

"Is that what he wants?"

"Probably not, knowing my father, but I don't know if he'll ever be fit enough to discuss it. Meanwhile, he has patients."

The phone rang again.

"When it quiets down, could you check it out?" asked Muffy.

Mrs. Lind nodded. "Dr. Sergeant's office, could you hold please?"

Muffy walked out to her car and drove to her own office. She knew she should call the hospital. Knew she should call Peter in case he left early. Instead, she set her briefcase on her desk, crossed the entry, and climbed the stairs.

She peeked into every door on the second floor. Whether for photography, sculpture, drawing, painting, or the children's summer crafts programs, all the rooms were in use.

Muffy trudged along the hall and opened the door to the third-floor stairs. Hot, stuffy air enveloped her. Up she climbed, sweat beading above her lips and down her spine.

At the top, a long straight hall cut the floor in half. Muffy began opening doors. Boxes filled the first and the racks of costumes and stage furnishings filled the second.

Across the hall, her steps echoed in the black-and-white tiled bath. She turned the sink taps. Clear water quickly followed rusty brown. She tested the other fixtures with the same result.

Closing the door on the functioning bath, she continued down the hall. At the end was an odd little room, wider than it was deep, with a tall bay window in the middle of the outside wall. Other than cobwebs draping the corners, it was empty. Small enough to cool with a new window unit. Electrical outlets rested on the high white baseboard of each wall, but there was no closet.

What will he do for clothes?

Muffy imagined Mrs. Pearlman waiting outside a men's fitting room, credit card in hand, while Peter emerged in suit, after tux, after jacket and slacks.

She imagined Peter sailing through a Goodwill store plucking any old T-shirt, shorts, and jeans off the racks and slapping them on the counter along with a twenty-dollar bill.

Muffy didn't see herself in either picture. She recalled his words.

"Gant. Did you lose your namesake, Peter? Will you feel as free as you said?"

She examined the little room one more time. The air conditioner would take some charm from the window, but there would still be plenty of light. She peered out the dusty panes and studied the angles of the shadows.

Northern light. That will work. He can use the kitchen downstairs. Actually, he can use the whole place. If he will.

She closed the door and retraced her steps. Coming out on the second floor felt like entering a freezer. She shivered as she mentally scoured her father's house for furniture, linens, and window coverings.

Before returning to her own office, she popped into Niki's.

"How's your dad?"

"Not good. We have an executive committee meeting tonight. Can you make a tentative agenda? You know most of the issues. Take all my calls, but if you see Consuela or Juan, send them in."

In her own office, Muffy hesitated to call her father, but she couldn't count on answers from the nurses' station. The few on the floor were so busy with paperwork they barely had time for the patients, let alone the families.

She dialed his cell phone. After two rings, she heard fumbling, then a weak, "Dr. Sergeant. Is this an emergency?"

"No. This is Alexandra. How are you?"

"I feel worse than patients I've seen in the morgue."

"What about the maternity slippers and the Cheshire cat?"

"I don't know what you're talking about."

"Well, that's good. You may feel awful, but you're better than yesterday. Get some rest. I'll be over soon."

"Take your time." He hung up without a good-bye.

At least he was better. She could pick up a signature card at the bank. Have him sign it. Get into the safe box. Find the will and certificates.

Okay. One down, one to go.

She found the number for the Strekers. It rang and rang. No answer. She felt hotter than she had on the third floor. She pressed redial. No answer. No answering machine. Were they sailing? Had he already left?

"Ma'am. You want to see me?" Consuela poked her head in the door.

"Yes. Come in. You said maybe you would continue working, after your move. Can you do that?"

"Sí."

"Good. Not sure how much we can pay you, but I'll talk to the board. Today, I need your help upstairs. Third floor. The bath and the room at the end of the hall. Give them a thorough cleaning. Especially the windows. Open them if you can."

"Yes, ma'am." Consuela nodded, backed out the door, and closed it.

Muffy tried the Strekers again. Still no answer. She pressed the intercom for Niki and then turned on her computer.

"Do you have Juan and Consuela on the agenda?"

"I do."

"Good. I'll be here for about ten minutes, then I'm going to the bank and hospital."

She considered having Niki keep Strekers on redial until someone answered, but she needed, and wanted, to speak to Peter herself.

"If Peter Gant. . . ."

"That new figure teacher?"

"The very one. If he comes while I'm gone, call me immediately. Drop everything. Keep him with you. I'll return right away."

"Oooh. So it's that serious," Niki teased.

"Yes. No. I'll explain the whole thing tomorrow."

The day was racing by in a blur and dragging her with it. She noticed that she had spoken of her father without crying. Had those tears released her grief? Or was her soul simply making room for more?

Muffy called up the Wachovia Bank web site and entered her pin for The Arts Center account. In the checking account, there was enough money for the month's budgeted bills. In the savings account, there was a little more than what was required for the major-account perks.

There were no CDs, no bonds, and no linked endowment account. No extra money for Juan and Consuela or a new window air conditioner.

As the printer produced copies of the account activity for the last month, Muffy pushed redial for the Strekers. Still no answer.

When she entered Dr. Sergeant's room with the safe box signature card tucked in her bag, he was sleeping. His face was as pale as the pillow. The bag hanging from the IV pole looked empty. She wanted to check his chart and feel his forehead, but she didn't want to wake him. Some nurse or aide would do that soon enough.

As she stood staring at him, a young man she'd never seen came into the room. She lifted her eyebrows to silently question his presence. He glanced at the sleeping man and then motioned Muffy into the hall.

He looked more like a football player than a doctor. His head was shaved and his dark eyes flickered between enthusiastic and concerned. Although his clothes were fashionable and finely tailored, they were closer to sport casual than smart casual.

He held out a warm, firm hand. "I'm Mark Pfeiffer. Dr. Mark Pfeiffer," he amended with pride. "Are you Dr. Sergeant's daughter?"

"Yes. Alexandra." She knit her brows. "Are you a specialist?"

"No. Family medicine. I just finished my residency at Jefferson in Philly. Um, I heard that Dr. Sergeant might be looking . . . Um, might be needing someone. . . ." He sighed.

So used to studying, diagnosing, and prescribing, he had no idea how to promote himself. Fortunately, he'd unconsciously got the basics right. Look well-groomed and smile.

"I'm not sure he will ever be well enough to practice again," Muffy whispered. "He will at least need a partner, if not someone to take over his practice. Do you have a card? References? Credentials we can review?"

"Not with me. I thought maybe I could speak with him, but it doesn't look like that's going to happen."

Muffy shook her head. "Not today. Get me your paperwork. I'll speak to him. If everything's in order, and he's up to it, we'll arrange a meeting. Could you start immediately?"

Dr. Pfeiffer nodded. "I'd like to see the office. I spoke with Mrs. Lind on the phone, but I'd like to meet her."

"Sure. It's right in town." She gave him the address and directions.

"Housing?" he asked. "I've got a room in Philly right now. I go month to month. Are there condos in town?"

Muffy pictured the windows above the little shops. Mark Pfeiffer didn't fit. "I'm sure you can find something near Longwood. For now. My father's practice earns a nice living. A younger, vibrant man could certainly build it."

Dr. Pfeiffer beamed.

"Fax your papers to me at The Arts Center and I'll check them this afternoon." She gave him her card, received a hardy handshake, and watched him hurry for the elevator.

Before returning to her father's bedside, she tried the Strekers once more. Heather answered. Muffy's heart pounded in her throat.

"Hi. It's Muffy. Is Peter there?"

Chapter Fourteen

"Well, fair Muffy, I missed you this morning."

Muffy cherished his merry voice, hoping her own would not betray her. "Where've you been?" she asked.

"Swimming."

"All morning?"

"After the sitting. They went sailing. I went swimming. I had enjoyed swimming alone. Until yesterday."

His voice turned to a whisper. "Shall I tell them we must return next weekend so I can finish the portrait here?"

For only an instant, Muffy let herself picture a moonlight swim. Immediately, a picture of burned rubble replaced it.

"Are you still returning today?" she asked, in an unintended business voice. She forced herself to smile. "I mean, I don't want to wait a week. I want to see you today. Can you meet me at The Arts Center and come back for dinner? I've already told Grace to cook for us."

Silence.

Muffy held her breath and then babbled, "I've found some sheer curtains, maybe you could show me how to drape them."

"I can," he finally answered. "I should let Mrs. Pearlman know. I told her—"

"I'll call her," Muffy blurted out too fast. "She wanted to discuss your career with me."

Again, he was silent.

"How's the portrait coming?" she asked.

"Fine. What time do you eat?"

"Six. Can you be here by five-thirty?"

"I'll have Heather drop me off. Could you give me a ride to Paoli?"

Now it was Muffy's turn to consider her answer. "Yes. I'll see you soon."

She closed her phone, wondering if she should bring him to the meeting. Staff members wheeling carts of supplies, equipment, and lunch trays passed her without a word. She glanced in at her father. His chin looked wooly as the sun shone on his unshaven face. His mouth hung open as he slept.

Quietly, she called Mrs. Pearlman and shared her plans. As she finished, she considered the board meeting. Would Henry Halliday be there? Evelyn Richardson would be. Would she object to the new resident?

"Alexandra?"

Muffy snapped back to the present and strode toward her father's bedside. He pressed the wrist with the plastic name band to his forehead. "Am I dying?" he asked.

She brought her own hand to his forehead. It felt warm but not hot.

"No. You have an infection, but the antibiotics have brought your fever down."

"It's no use. I can't have chemo with an infection."

"Father, you don't have to start chemo until you've recovered from surgery. You know that."

Muffy took his hand in hers, knowing he knew more than she could even suspect about his condition.

"They can treat the symptoms," he said, "but not the cause." His weary eyes looked up to hers. "I've left you a mess to deal with."

A compassionate smile relaxed her face.

"Fortunately, a simple business mess, Father. The kind I'm trained to fix."

Muffy gently released the hand she held and retrieved the

signature card from her bag. "There are papers I couldn't find in the desk," she said. "I assume they're in the safe box."

He nodded. "My will."

More than that, I hope.

"Would you sign this so I have access to it?"

He reached for the card and pen. "You'll need power of attorney too."

Muffy nodded as she tucked the card back into her bag. "Shall I interview some young docs to see your patients?"

Dr. Sergeant's flesh seemed to gray before Muffy finished the sentence. He slowly nodded, glanced at her, and closed his eyes.

"Get the power of attorney," he mumbled.

Muffy bent and kissed his warm forehead. "You rest. I'll take care of everything. When you come home, we'll have time for some fun. Some catching up."

He was already asleep.

On the way back from the hospital, she first stopped at the bank to empty the safe-deposit box and then at Strawbridge's department store. The blue, Oxford-cloth, button-down Gant shirt was not on sale. She set it on the cashier's counter with her American Express card on top.

"Would you like to open a Strawbridge's account and save ten percent?" the clerk asked.

"No, but I'd like this gift-wrapped. Is customer service still upstairs?"

The woman nodded as Muffy decided to save the ten percent bribe for the day she really needed it.

As the gift wrapper secured the green-and-gold-striped paper with streamers of tape, Muffy called her assistant and shared the story of the fire.

"I think The Center could use a resident artist. You agree?"

"Peter?"

Muffy described the third-floor rooms.

"Do you really think he'd settle for Chester County after living in Paoli?"

"If he's serious about his art, he'll need more inspiration than hothouse flowers."

"He's serious," said Niki. "At least that's what his students say. He expects art from them, not just pretty pictures. By the way, no one asked for a refund. Does he have references or do you think we'll need a background check?"

That could be a problem, depending how far back they look.

"Mrs. Pearlman would give him a good reference," said Muffy. "She wouldn't have a criminal watch her house."

"You've got a point."

When Muffy returned to The Arts Center, Dr. Pfeiffer's papers lay on her desk under a Post-It note bearing Niki's big red question mark.

By 5:00, she had the Pfeiffer papers highlighted along with a page of notes she'd taken from the references she'd called. The power-of-attorney form was ready to be signed and notarized. The Everest and Richfield Fund certificates were ready for Halliday and a copy of Dr. Sergeant's living will was ready for the hospital.

Muffy slid her feet into her boring beige heels and checked her watch. Peter burst through her doorway filling her office with vacation air and a mischievous grin.

"I'm on time," he announced.

Muffy had to smile. "So you are. Wonderful. Are you hungry?"

"Always. May I give you a hug if I close the door, or would you get fired?"

Before she could answer, he guided the door to its jamb, and Muffy to his arms. She felt the sun on his skin and smelled the sea in his shirt. In his arms, all the chaos of her life seemed to disappear.

She raised her head and he touched her mouth with a kiss as gentle as a moth's wing on spider silk.

Slowly he released her.

"Peter, I'd like to show you something."

"A birthmark? Don't worry. I just won't paint it."

You sweet man. So full of fun. I'm going to tell you you've lost everything and then offer you a hot, stuffy consolation prize.

She touched his arm and reached for her door. She said nothing as they climbed the two flights. His eyes were still merry when she opened the door to his prospective new home.

Consuela had earned her keep. The clean, open windows allowed a warm breeze and soft light to fill the room. The hardwood floors were washed and polished; the white plaster walls were dust and cobweb free.

Muffy stared up at him. Let him guess. At least part of it.

"Our new home?" he asked.

Muffy opened her mouth. Words stayed in. Breath stayed out.

"Ours?" she whispered. Papers and portraits, parents and pottery didn't exist. For one exquisite moment the unit of Alexandra and Peter stood alone in the world. A warm, light, free, and easy world. One of laughter and kisses. A world she'd like to stay in forever.

She watched as he walked to the window, turned, and looked up at the high ceiling. His eyes returned to hers.

"There was a fire," he said. "Did you see it on the news?"

The free and easy world disappeared.

"A fire?" she asked. "At the shore?"

He shook his head. "The carriage house. Burned to the ground."

Muffy searched his eyes for sadness, worry, fear, or regret. She found nothing but the Peter she'd known since James's party.

"Yes," she answered. "Mrs. Pearlman called. I told her I'd tell you." She took a breath. "You've lost everything."

"Meant to be." He grinned.

Muffy shook her head. *What is he thinking? How can he be happy? Did he plan the fire? Will he burn The Arts Center? I truly don't know him.*

"What?" he asked, reading her expression.

"How can you be so . . . happy?"

Now he frowned. "What can I do about it?"

"Nothing, but . . ."

"I've lost replaceable art books, worn-out clothes, ten years of sketchbooks I never refer to, a used bike, and a chaise longue no one wanted at the auction but me."

"Did you plan it?" The question was in the air before she could catch it.

"No. Arson was one crime Glen Mills didn't accept. Before the new director, there was a fire. Boys died. Why would you even think that?"

Ashamed of herself but still confused, Muffy dropped her head and walked toward the window.

"You've spoken with Mrs. Pearlman?" she asked.

"Yeah."

Muffy cleared her throat, wishing she had more facts to work with instead of a mere warm feeling. Her business self took command.

"If you don't want to stay in Paoli, I can offer you this room. I'll need board approval. There's northern light and a bath down the hall. Kitchen downstairs."

"But," he answered, "I might either burn the place down or expect you to bring me home for dinner every night."

She cringed at his perceptiveness.

"The room's perfect," he said. "How's your dad?"

Muffy's head spun. There didn't seem to be a vindictive bone in this man's body. But what did she know?

She took a breath. "He's better, but it may be simply a window before he gets worse."

She checked her watch. "Mrs. Gazner gets grouchy when I'm late." The words rang in Muffy's head along with years of Grace's scolding. She gritted her teeth.

"Actually, I'm sick and tired of Grace Gazner and her snippy, snotty attitude. And I have a board meeting tonight. You can come with me. I'll introduce you and present my idea first. If you're interested."

"I'll need a car."

"You can use mine. For now. Drive it back tonight. I don't know when the meeting will finish. . . . Oh, Peter, I don't know you at all. I don't understand how you think. How you run your life. But . . . you make me feel so good. And you paint so well."

Peter took her hand and led her back to her office.

"Let's go see what Grouchy Grace has cooked up. While we eat, you can interview me. Fair enough?"

At the Sergeant residence, bold Peter marched into the kitchen and lifted the lid on the steamer. "Perfect," he said to a startled Grace. "It's too late for good asparagus."

Then he bent over and examined her face. "Great bones are wasted on girls. They keep a woman looking elegant forever." He winked. Grace blushed. Muffy took his arm and led him back to the dining room.

Peter paused and studied the busy dollhouse painting. "If this were a video game, you'd clear out the people, add twenty stories, and hide the key in a drawer in the card table."

He turned and smiled. "But it's not a game. It's a wonderful place to visit, isn't it?"

Muffy thought of all the lonely meals she'd eaten in this room with only those painted people for company. She nodded.

"Sit here," she said, indicating her father's chair.

As they sat, Grace brought dishes of steamed snap peas, cold poached salmon, and tiny new red potatoes. She smiled at Peter. "Are there any condiments you need?" she asked.

"Condiments mask the flavor of well-prepared food. Thank you."

Muffy rolled her eyes, but smiled.

After Grace returned to the kitchen, he asked, "What do you want to know?"

So many questions whirled in her mind that her mouth froze.

"Let me start," he said. "What's your favorite color, Ms. Sergeant? Beige?"

Muffy slid a group of peas into a line and cut them in half with one stroke. "I guess all little girls like pink. When my mother died, my father began choosing my clothes. And even when he didn't, I automatically chose what he would have. Tell me about your flower paintings."

"An exercise. I was playing with real light, palettes. Purple's my favorite color, but I haven't used it in years. I bought some dioxazine purple and manganese violet. Not much call for purples except for flowers and robes. I was playing, getting back into painting, but Mrs. Pearlman jumped in. Thought I should show. Didn't think of your Ms. Richardson. She's on your board, right?"

"We'll get around her. Niki says your students are impressed. What kind of games did you make?"

He described castles and monsters and aides for the hero in his quest. Then he hummed a tune and danced his fingers up to the next level of the game.

"Ah, saved the princess." He grinned. "Every night, I'd go to sleep with wall textures and receding floors in my head. Ever play?"

"My father thought it was a waste of time."

"It is." He chuckled. "It's a vacation without leaving your chair."

"Have you traveled?" she asked.

"Just to Germany. I wanted to see real castles."

Muffy looked at her plate. Empty. She hadn't tasted a thing. She looked at Peter's. Half full.

"I'm sorry," she said. "Please eat. I'll tell you about The Arts Center."

As she told of the Havilands, Jake Waite's endowment, and the art program, she grew increasingly uncomfortable. "I'm boring us both to death."

She brought her glass to her lips and finished her water.

Peter set his utensils across his empty plate. "What's your mission?" he asked.

"To provide the community with opportunities for artistic expression and enjoyment," she recited. "Even that sounds so boring. Grace," she called.

* * *

Peter sat in a chair near the door while Muffy called the executive committee meeting to order. Package folds creased his new, blue Gant shirt but it presented a more polished resident artist than the AxshunArtz Princess T-shirt.

"Please meet Peter Cinnsealaigh who paints as Peter Gant."

She glanced at Evelyn Richardson who was studying the agenda, and then presented her idea and highlights of Peter's background. She included the fire, omitted Glen Mills.

"Do you have any questions for Peter?" she asked.

"You have references?" asked Martin Sinclair.

"I do." Peter stood. "Elane Pearlman. Northrop Kingston."

At the mention of Kingston, heads nodded with a hum of approval.

"What will you give The Center besides an after-hours presence?" Evelyn asked, peering over her half-lens glasses.

"Critiques. Newsletter column. Curriculum ideas. A show."

She made tiny notes on her agenda.

Muffy scanned the quiet members. "Thank you, Peter."

He nodded and left, her car keys in his pocket.

Before the board got tangled up discussing the prospective resident and Henry Halliday could excuse himself, Muffy asked him, "Where's the endowment?"

Halliday was prepared. He gave each board member a thick, detailed, fine-print copy of the prospectus for each of the funds he'd chosen. "As you know, past performance is no guarantee of future returns, but look at these numbers and tell me where else you could invest the assets of this thriving institution and be better prepared to harvest the gains of the next bull market."

"We are in a bear market," said Muffy.

"Our little lady is so astute." He smirked. "I have invested your stagnant money in funds that are on sale. You ladies know what I'm talking about. I've seen all of you at the Talbots' after-Christmas sale when I go with Marge. Stock funds are the same. You need to buy low, then take your profits."

"Mr. Halliday, where does the money come from for next month's bills?" asked Muffy.

"You've got plenty with your savings and classes and memberships. Current income, Muffy dear."

Muffy looked from one board member to the next. She saw confusion, boredom, and impatience. No allies.

"Very well, Mr. Halliday, let's compare last month's payables against receivables, as well as those of last July."

"Oh, Muffy," groaned Evelyn, "is this really necessary? Can't you and Henry do this in a committee and then simply give us a report?"

"Yes," said Halliday.

"No," said Muffy as she looked around the table for even one pair of sympathetic eyes. "You, all of you, were elected to ensure that The Arts Center would be a thriving organization the entire community could be proud of. When The Center stops paying its bills, all of our names will be in the paper."

She stared at Henry. "Will that be good business for Halliday and Crawford?"

"Muffy, Muffy, Muffy. Such a well-educated girl but so lacking in experience."

"Henry, that's enough," said Martin Sinclair. "You and I will follow Evelyn's suggestion and work this out in our own committee. I'll have a report for you by Friday, Muffy. Okay?"

"Thank you Mr. Sinclair. Now that you've all had a few minutes to consider our resident artist. . . ."

Chapter Fifteen

When Muffy parked the car under the portico, lightning bugs hovered over the hedge. Brilliantly, intermittently, they flashed their availability.

She sat watching them in her father's air-conditioned, leather-lined cocoon. A firefly landed on the windshield. Its body brightened and then dimmed. She pictured the flute and curtains waiting in the music room. The firefly glowed again.

Well, Peter, the board approved. Will you still feel so warm and merry if I see you every day?

Her mouth spread into a smile.

Will you ever earn enough money to live on? Will you want to?

The firefly lifted off the glass and floated toward the tiny lights hovering above the hedge. Muffy opened the car and pulled out her bags. When she entered the house, she smelled baking.

He's even put a spell on Grace.

She couldn't help but smile as she snuck into the kitchen. On the counter, a platter full of peanut butter cookies snuggled under a blanket of plastic wrap. Quietly, she set her bags on the table. Silently, she lifted the wrap. She couldn't remember homemade cookies in the house since her mother died. That little house cookie jar had simply vanished, like the flute.

Oh Grace, would you have been a Mrs. Roberts if we'd charmed you? Or did you need Peter?

I need Peter. Or is it want? Does it matter?

Muffy nibbled the nutty delight. From the pad by the phone, she ripped a sheet and printed: *Delicious! Thanks, Grace.* She left it on the counter.

After slipping out of her long, busy day, Muffy sat in her cluttered room, knees bent under her pink flowered sheets. It felt strange to be so alone in this huge house. When her father was merely having surgery, she could think of her nights alone as vacation time. Now, she wondered if he would ever sleep here again.

When she saw him after the board meeting, he had slipped in and out of their conversation. His big news was clear liquids, the first step toward real meals.

She didn't feel his forehead. Couldn't discreetly hold his hand. Couldn't divine his temperature. Twice, she tried to introduce the idea of Dr. Pfeiffer. No go.

Niki was a notary. She would come and witness the power of attorney signatures, if her father were lucid in the morning.

She picked up her cell phone and set it back down. Peter's hadn't burned, but it would ring somewhere in Mrs. Pearlman's house.

How would I feel if a fire burned everything I owned?

She let her clothes and bedroom furniture go up in mental flames. She rescued her great grandmother's pink-flowered porcelain clock, her grandmother's velvet crazy quilt, and her mother's flute.

"My family. All I have left of it. And if I'd never had a family, would anything have meaning for me?"

She thought about the boxes of Wedgwood and Limoges in the attic. The unused silver in the dining room.

"I love big parties. All the people having fun, dressed so nicely, meeting each other, making new friends, enjoying delicious foods. Arts Center parties. Not little dinner parties. Peter loves parties too."

Her phone rang. She answered on the first ring.

"Is it you?" he asked.

She had to smile. "Who else would it be?"

He chuckled.

"You are welcome to reside at The Arts Center," she said. "The board agrees we need a presence. But no wild parties I'm not invited to. No beer cans strewn all over the ballroom."

He answered immediately and seriously. "As your resident artist, I'll need to have a work on display in your foyer."

He's coming. He'll really live at The Center. He'll be in my mornings, and in my evenings.

"Muffy?"

"Sorry." Grinning, she said, "Yes. Your work on display. A show. Critiques. A column. What did you mean about curriculum?"

"You need a more exciting mission. Did you get your financial mess fixed?"

She explained how Martin Sinclair had understood her warning and intervened.

"It'll be a few days before we can get the room furnished," she added.

"No problem. How's your dad?"

"I don't know. He kept dozing. I didn't stay long. I got there late."

She told him about Dr. Pfeiffer, the safe-deposit box, and the power of attorney as if they hadn't seen each other at dinner. But dinner had been a foundation-laying time, not a forum for personal current events.

After saying good night, she set the phone on the bedside table and switched out the light.

After saying good night, Peter fished his faded, blue Gant shirt from his bag and carried it across the carpeted hall. In the pristine bath, he prepared to rinse his Rehoboth Beach days down the drain.

Muffy's phone rang at 4:30 A.M.

"Miss Sergeant?"

"Yes."

"This is Central County Medical. Sorry to wake you. Your father's not good."

"I'll be right there."

Muffy threw on gray slacks and a cream top. Grabbed a mauve jacket; slid into black flats. She whipped a hairbrush through her hair and toothbrush around her mouth.

She stood at her father's bedside in ICU just after 5:00.

Behind white curtains, tubes of fluids and wires to monitors surrounded the old doctor. He lay alone. Muffy pictured a remote nurse watching a bank of screens for warnings of the disasters she would rush to prevent.

For a moment, Muffy watched her father breathe. There was a new, plastic tube draped around his ears with two tiny fingers pointing into his nostrils. Oxygen. Dark tubing drooped from under the sheet to drag on the floor again.

The bedside tray stood between them. She swung it toward the curtain. "Father," she whispered. She took his hand. Hot. Without opening his eyes, he turned his head. The nosepiece failed to follow. One of the tiny fingers now aimed the air at his eye.

Muffy laid his hand on the white, cotton blanket and marched to the nurses' station. "Excuse me," she said to the cluster of women behind the counter. "Why is my father on oxygen?"

"He's got pneumonia," answered the woman in a tunic with little angels sitting on puffy white clouds.

"He moved and the nosepiece didn't," said Muffy. "Also, there's a tube on the floor. Isn't that a good way for bacteria to enter the body?" Anger began coating her words. "If this is the way you care for a doctor, how can any of the rest of us hope to get out of here alive?"

The woman wearing the angels glanced at her cronies. "I'll check on him," she said.

Muffy followed her to Dr. Sergeant's bedside. Without a word, the woman adjusted the nosepiece. After she left, Muffy stood watching her father's shallow breaths. There was no chair.

You are all the family I have left.

Muffy sat on the foot of the bed. The thin blanket pulled away from his chin. The grey stubble had grown longer.

Staring down at her mismatched clothes, she recalled Peter's first words to her. "Wrong dress, but you're gorgeous."

Not now.

She glanced back at her father and was surprised to see his eyes open. "Father?"

"Alexandra."

"You feeling better?"

As he turned his head, the nosepiece popped loose again. Muffy grasped his hand and held her breath. Alexander released his. He didn't take another.

She waited, watching the light leave his eyes. Raising his warm hand to her lips, she kissed him good-bye.

The next two days both rushed and stalled in a blur of making lists and phone calls, reading cards and memos, trying to eat and sleep.

While Peter taught, Muffy selected a casket. While he positioned the easel displaying the Strekers, she chose pallbearers.

She arrived at the funeral home early for the viewing. Dim lights, quiet hymns, and enormous bouquets of roses seemed to fill every inch of the long, open room. The same room where Maddy's Muffin had said a final good-bye to her mommy.

Muffy took a deep breath of the useless air and blew it back into the room. It would be such a luxury to have Peter take her hand and lead her to the coffin. Put his arm around her waist and be her comfort while she faced every living soul she knew.

Peering out into the parking lot, she saw the first cars arriving. Turning her back, she marched to her place at Dr.

Sergeant's feet. And there she stood in her plain, black dress, greeting her father's patients, friends, and adversaries for the next two hours.

The only time she cried was when James, Leah, and Mrs. Roberts enveloped her in a group hug. She had the courage to look Leah straight in the eye for the first time.

"I'm sorry I was such a witch."

"It's okay," Leah said.

Muffy looked up at James. "Thanks for coming, old friend."

She searched her heart. James was truly a dear, old friend now. Nothing more. Peter was the man her heart longed for.

"How's Peter?" asked James.

Before Muffy could answer, Leah did. "He's thrilled. Excited about the move. Surprised he likes teaching. He said this is the beginning of his real career."

Muffy nodded, pretending she knew all this. She realized she'd been too full of her own life to hear about his.

Mrs. Roberts took her hand. "If you need anything at all, dear, you just call. Promise?"

Muffy nodded, and then patients took the places of her friends. "If it weren't for your father. . . ."

"You know his second opinion saved. . . ."

"He was gruff, but. . . ."

Hearing stories of recovery and reluctant compassion, she replayed scenes of her own life with the doctor. In each, she was forced to revise her opinion of the father she thought she knew.

As the last guest slipped out the door, Muffy turned to the man reclining on satin pillows. "Goodbye, Father," she whispered. As she memorized the nose and chin she'd never see again, she heard a page flip in the guest book.

Turning, she saw Peter bent over the walnut podium. Outrageous clothes, but they fit him perfectly. From the costume closet, he'd borrowed the long-tailed black coat and pants of Dolly Cusins from *Major Barbara.*

When he met her eyes, he nodded but didn't smile. She wanted to run to him, grab his hand, and keep going out the door. She wanted to run to him, bury her head in his coat, and cry. She stood motionless.

In long, silent strides he joined her, kissed her forehead, and put his arm around her waist. "Are you okay?" he asked.

"No. But it helps that you're here."

They stared at the figure reclining in the casket.

"You have his ears," said Peter.

She bent closer, studied the perfect curves, and then put a hand to her own ear. *I do. Thank you, Father. I never thought I'd be grateful to have any part of you. But we do share beautiful ears.*

She turned to Peter but he was addressing Dr. Sergeant. "I would ask you for your daughter's hand, sir, but my timing's a little off."

Muffy froze. She couldn't breathe. Couldn't meet his eyes. Couldn't let him see how seriously she'd taken his joke. She needed to laugh. Smile. Something.

Peter continued. "I'll take excellent care of Alexandra. Not the kind you'd take, but I'll make sure she has fun." He looked down at Muffy and wrapped her in his arms.

For a long moment she basked in that warm, protective cove, wondering what his words really meant. The last time she'd seen him, she could ask him anything. Now something had shifted. The answers would matter too much.

He had not asked her to marry him, only told her dead father he would have asked his permission. It was only a wish, not a proposal.

He released her.

Before her nagging mind could continue to ruin the evening, he whispered, "My place, or yours?"

"Yours?"

"Great idea. I'll meet you there."

"Where?"

"Third floor, end of the hall."

Muffy drove out to The Arts Center in a daze. Was he sleeping on the bare floor or a pile of costumes? Did he have keys? Should he really be trusted?

She parked her father's big dark Mercedes beside her own bright BMW. Peter dashed up the slate steps and turned the key in the lock as if he'd done it all his life. He held the door as she entered and flipped on the golden glass sconces. It felt weird to have someone else act the host in the space she'd controlled for years.

The four Streker Chandler women smiled from the canvas in the entry hall. They looked so real that Muffy half expected them to wave and call, "Welcome." Up close, she could see the tiny brush strokes. She backed away. What she'd seen at Rehoboth had looked nearly finished; now it seemed as crude as a sketch.

"How did you do it?" she asked.

Peter grinned. "I just paint what I see, ma'am. Have you eaten?"

"Oh, I should have brought you some. The whole town has brought food. Have you eaten?"

"I'm good." He grasped her hand and bounded up the great stairs, coattails flying behind him.

The third floor seemed even hotter than it had the day of her last visit. The hall was dark. All the doors were closed. With a hand on her waist, he led her to the end of the hall.

"Close your eyes," he said.

She almost feared that her step over his threshold would be a step into a dark abyss. Putting her hands over her eyes, she had something to cling to even if it were no more substantial than her own face.

"Look!"

She held her breath, removed her hands and relaxed. The entire window wall was covered with white linen drapes. A new air conditioner quietly cooled the air. Two torchier lamps bounced light from the white ceiling onto a purple comforter covering a double bed.

On the other side of the room, a nicked and chipped paint-spattered table held jars of brushes and tubes of paint.

Peter touched the black box on the armoire tucked away in

the corner. Music replaced the air conditioner's hum, hinting at dancing and drifting to dreamland.

"Where did all this come from?" she asked.

"Your generous members. And Mrs. Pearlman. Wait here."

Peter dashed back into the hot hall. He returned in an instant with two icy bottles. Twisting off each cap, he handed Muffy one cola and kept the other. "Can't run the fridge and the air conditioner on the same circuit."

Clinking his bottle to hers, he said, "Here's to Alex Sergeant, who fathered the most gorgeous woman in the world."

Muffy hadn't realized how thirsty she was until the soda wet her tongue. She swallowed and held her bottle to Peter's. "And here's to my life as an orphan. Will you show me how to do it?"

"The first thing you'll need to do is get rid of those awful clothes."

Chapter Sixteen

Muffy glanced warily at the closed drapes, wondering if her silhouette would be visible to the entire town and The Arts Center board.

"Not tonight," said Peter. "You're tired. I just wanted you to see my new home, and to thank you. Niki's featuring me in your July newsletter. Portraits, critiques, classes—"

"Classes? You told me you didn't want to teach."

"When I had to drive, it was a waste of time. Now with the contacts, it's a good idea."

"Oh." Somehow Muffy felt eclipsed. She used to make the major decisions here and delegate the rest. Now, in two days, it seemed like Niki and Peter were running the whole place.

Your father died. You were busy.

But I thought Peter would need me to promote him. . . . He already knows how.

Peter set his soda on the paint table and laid his hands on her shoulders. His fingers sought out the tight chords supporting her head full of heavy thoughts. Reluctantly, she leaned into his chest. He still radiated that calm warmth. Gradually, he persuaded the knots in her neck to let go.

"I found some wonderful fabric in the costume room," he whispered.

"Mmm?"

He held her shoulders away from him. "Would you still pose for me?"

"Will you come to the funeral and the open house with me?"

Peter accompanied her through that long next day. Muffy was skilled at festive events and witty conversation; she was inept at sad gatherings and morose small talk.

Between the hymns, the procession to the cemetery, and old friends' stories about the doctor, she wondered what would fill the void her father had left. How would she survive on her modest salary? Could The Arts Center afford even that?

When the last guest left the Sergeant home, she left Grace in the kitchen and led Peter to her father's office. She offered him a leather chair and then sat down at her father's desk.

He walked to the bookcases holding the doctor's collection of antique medical instruments. She watched as he studied the huge syringes and rusty tweezers.

"What's this?" he asked, picking up a fan of dull brass knives.

"A bloodletter."

"You know." He sighed. "I wouldn't even use these in a still life."

Muffy pictured her father surrounded by all these old, ugly devices. Then she pictured him taking his last breath surrounded by all those new, ugly devices. And over that image lay the tender moment when Peter compared their ears and asked for her hand.

He settled into the client's chair beside the desk. "You can let your hair down now," he said.

"First I want you to hear this." She lifted the light blue paper cover of the will. "Upon my death, all my assets are to be sold and the proceeds placed in the established trust of Alexandra Madeleine Sergeant."

She laid the paper on the blotter. "That means everything except my car will be sold and put into a trust I cannot touch until I'm thirty five."

"Bummer. What are you going to do?"

"I guess I'll have to learn how to be poor as well as how to be an orphan." With one great swish of her arm, the will and the rest of the doctor's papers went flying toward the floor.

"Who controls the trust?" asked Peter. "That crook on your board?"

Muffy nodded.

Peter rose and sat on the edge of the bare desk. He leaned toward her and cupped her face in his wide hands. With his thumb, he traced the tiny valley between her nose and her lip.

She took his hands in hers and held them inches from her lips. "Are you touching me, Peter, or figuring out shadows and colors?"

He drew her hands to his own lips and kissed them. The green eyes fixed on hers didn't twinkle or measure. He slid from the desk and pulled her from the chair. After kissing her fingers, he placed her palms against his cheeks.

"Some guy controls your money. Some woman controls my heart. In five years, you'll control your money. You have it in writing. And my heart? That's in your hands."

He dropped his hands, but not his eyes. She stroked his cheekbones, then rose to her toes to touch her lips to his. His arms encircled her, pressed her close.

She relaxed. The energy in his touch, and especially his kiss, seemed to fill those reservoirs within her that the funeral day had drained.

She broke the kiss, slid her hands to his chest, and tucked her head beneath his chin.

Whatever this wonderful energy is, he simply gives it. I can take all I need. And it doesn't seem like he misses it. Is this love?

"Peter?"

She leaned back and gazed into his eyes.

"Does it feel good when I kiss you?"

His face split into a grin.

Muffy tipped her head and looked through her lashes. "I mean . . . I mean, do you feel warm inside?"

Laughter rolled from his shoulders and chest. "It's called hot, Muffy."

"No. That's not what I meant."

"Right. Yes, actually dear, I do feel a trifle warm. Perhaps it's the weather."

"Never mind," she said.

He gathered her back into his arms and kissed the top of her head. "Thinking of you warms my heart, but touching you feels like cadmium scarlet."

The next day, Muffy met Martin Sinclair for lunch at PJ's, a cottage made into a cats-in-pajamas-themed restaurant on the bank of the Brandywine River.

Under the gaze of a tall statue cat dressed in red silk pajamas, Muffy sipped her ice water as Sinclair twisted the lemon peel into his drink.

"Well, I finally nailed Halliday down yesterday afternoon," he said. "It's messier than I thought. The guy's slick. I thought he was giving you the runaround . . . young female and all that." He took a sip.

"I couldn't get a straight answer either. Hope you don't mind; I've called a board meeting for tomorrow. We've got to vote him off and force him to hand over all the papers he has."

Muffy crushed an ice chip between her teeth. She hadn't thought she could feel worse. Would Peter have to leave her life before she finally hit bottom?

She took a deep breath.

"Thanks, Martin. We'll need a replacement. And we need to fill my father's place."

"We need to save our skin first."

The waitress brought beautiful bowls heaped with greens and chilled seafood.

"Have you called our solicitor?" she asked.

"Forgot."

"I'll do it. What time's the meeting?"

"One. Griffin wants to get his golf in."

"What about Mr. Crawford? Is he in on this?"

Sinclair shrugged. "They're partners."

Muffy sighed and filled her mouth with fork after fork of salad, tasting nothing.

She spent the rest of the afternoon proofing the newsletter featuring the new resident artist, reviewing registrations for the second summer session of classes, and checking the dwindling bank account balances online.

It was after 5:00 when she closed and locked her office door. Through the side light at the front door, she watched Peter sketch the last of the pottery guild members as they tucked boxes of pots into their trunks. He wore a T-shirt with a huge, winking smiley face basking on his back.

Muffy smiled and some of the day's tension drifted down to the carpet for Consuela to vacuum away. She opened the heavy door and stepped into the sweltering afternoon.

"Hi," she said.

"Hi." He grinned. "Have a seat." He patted the slate steps. "What catastrophes have you collected today?"

Muffy settled herself and her bags down on the step by his side. He wrapped an arm around her shoulder and drew her close.

"I feel like quitting," she confessed.

He kissed her hair. "Go ahead."

She shook her head. "Don't you take anything seriously?"

"Just you."

Muffy remembered the contest and the mystery fabric in the costume room.

"Right. First, come help me eat some well-intentioned casseroles."

"No cakes? Pies? Cookies? You had loads of them yesterday. Did you eat them all?"

"Every bite."

Peter suddenly glanced past her, into the sky, and back to The Arts Center. "Perfect. I've got a pie in my fridge," he said, popping off the step. "Come."

Sublime Recline 141

Thirty minutes later, Muffy lay in a white gown on the window seat at the top of the stairs. The low sun backlit her golden hair. Tomorrow he'd add the flute. Today, he'd draped the mystery fabric over pillows supporting her limbs. The blue-violet velvet contrasted with the fair skin of Muffy's bare arms and legs.

"Fabric's fun to paint," he said. "Nice to look at. Easy to judge. Makes a picture look real. Dali, Chardin . . . masters."

"Dali?" All she could recall were images of distorted limbs.

"There's more fabric than flesh in his *Sacrament of the Last Supper*."

The filmy white dress from *A Midsummer's Night Dream* was a little snug in the bust, a little loose in the waist, but it didn't matter. Lying with one knee bent and both forearms raised, the costume became a gossamer veil hiding her torso.

A divine-looking Alexandra reclined on a sublime dais before a setting sun, a nymph innocently charming the gods with her golden music.

Peter stood behind the canvas painting the lightest lights and darkest darks into the sketch he'd drawn.

The lemon meringue pie remained in the fridge. Muffy relaxed into his pillows, allowing the dividers in her mind to open and the events of the last four days to mingle.

Despite Henry Halliday's greedy commission and the falling stock market, the funds were fundamentally solid and would come back in time. Despite the fact that her money would be inaccessible for five years, she had a good education and experience.

She could support herself. But The Arts Center might have to use principal to keep going. It might ask her to donate her time.

Dr. Pfeiffer seemed good enough and eager enough to take over the practice, but could he afford it?

And Peter. *"I was going to ask you for her hand, but my timing's a little off."* *Was that because my father was dead, or do you need to be successful first?*

She didn't know; couldn't tell. He seemed as comfortable dressed in a tux driving Mrs. Pearlman's Rolls Royce as he did sitting in the sand in a worn-out, thrift-store T-shirt.

"Done," he announced.

Muffy stretched. "Can I see?"

"Absolutely not. Light's gone for tonight. Are you free tomorrow? Same time?"

She nodded. "When things settle down, I've got to start flute lessons."

"You don't have a music program here, do you? Just art and theater?"

Immediately, Muffy's mind began sorting the mansion's space, adding sound-absorbing partitions, interviewing musicians, and writing proposals for the board. Then she remembered. Austerity budget.

"The timing's a little off," she said, studying his face for explanations those words might trigger.

"Timing's almost everything," he said. "Except for persistence and talent and who you know." He dropped his palette into the plastic box and snapped the lid shut.

"My pie or yours?"

Peter apologized for being bad company at the Sergeant dining table. He didn't notice the food going into his mouth. He forced himself to coddle Mrs. Gazner. The Muffy in his painting kept overriding the real one. He knew she knew it. He couldn't help it. He had to get back to his work.

At his insistence, Muffy returned him to The Arts Center.

"I don't need a car now," he said. "I'll pick up a bike this weekend."

After a quick kiss, he dashed inside and locked the door behind him. Alone in his studio/living room/bedroom/dining room, he turned on all the lights and studied the canvas. He puttered, making tiny corrections to lines and shadows and hues.

When he could paint no more without seeing the model, he pushed "play" and filled the air with the music.

He slumped on the bed. For the first time in a long time he began running expenses and income through his mind. He reached for the pad and pencil on the headboard. Soon, he was lost in the curves of the 2 and the 6, oblivious to the dollars they represented.

His cell phone rang. He had neither clock nor watch.

"Peter Gant here."

"It is I!"

"No."

Chris laughed. "Fine. I'll find another artist for my portrait. Really, you think you can escape us just by moving out here?"

"I'd hoped."

"You failed, buddy. We're on your doorstep. Get yourself down here."

Peter had to smile. As much as he loved making real art, he missed his friends.

When he opened the door, Chris and Mike were sitting on the slate steps in the glow of the wrought-iron, reproduction streetlight. They rose. Chris still looked like he never ate and Mike's eyes hid behind thick glasses.

"I'd ask you in, but my lease forbids wild parties," he said.

"Thanks anyway," said Chris. "No offense, but the place looks creepy."

Peter turned toward the mansion, checking for ghosts and gargoyles. "It's your creepy imagination," he said, following them to the red Corvette.

"That creepy imagination made us all a few bucks. And it'll make us a lot more. Where do you go around here?"

Peter directed them to Bentley's Inn, a dark cave of wood-paneled walls and wide-plank floors. The air was cool, but it felt like all the life had been breathed out weeks ago, leaving only a residue of stale exhalations.

While waiting for their drinks, Peter's eye was drawn to the watercolor riding scene above their table. Pedestrian. After he finished the painting of Muffy, he'd start on the work for his show. His first real show since PAFA. No flowers.

"Just listen," said Chris after the waitress had set down the glasses.

"No," said Peter. "You still don't understand. There's this contest . . ." He told them the whole story. He tried to describe Muffy as his model, but his friends read his tone.

"Petey's in love," teased Mike as he pushed his glasses up yet again.

"I've got a shot at my life's dream," said Peter. "Fine art. Ever hear of it?"

"Okay," said Chris, nodding at Mike. "Got the duct tape?"

Mike stood and pulled a roll of wide, gray tape from his pocket. "Sorry friend." He tried to scowl at Peter. "We don't want to use this, but we will if we have to."

Peter grinned and put up his hand.

Mike sat and set the tape on the table out of Peter's reach. "All we need are the initial renderings. We've got animators to fill in the rest. You can pretend it's fine art. No castles this time."

"It's a puzzle adventure game," said Chris.

"Space theme?" asked Peter.

"No," the friends answered together. "Real scenes. Ultra real. Places people want to spend time." Words ricocheted between the partners as they told the back story and set the scenes.

Peter brought his glass to his mouth. Their excitement charged the air. It was contagious. As they described caves and islands and fantastic vehicles, Peter's hand twitched. Before he knew it, he was reaching for a napkin.

Muffy's painter watched from a corner of his mind as Peter sketched and laughed. When he'd filled the napkins, a small sketch pad appeared on the table. As always, the three were in tune and used each new idea to generate more. Evenings like this had been some of the best of Peter's life. It felt like he imagined a family to be.

It was late when the three sat, spent, and lifted their warm drinks.

"You got me," said Peter.

"You coming back?" asked Mike. "We've got a great office in King of Prussia."

Peter laughed. "You guys are jerks. There is no place near here with worse traffic. When do you get there? Three in the morning?"

"That's when we leave," said Chris. "We go in after dinner."

"You coming back?" Mike repeated.

"You guys didn't hear a word I said."

The partners exchanged looks. "You didn't hear yourself either, friend."

Peter slid his chair back. "I'll bill you for tonight's work."

Later, as he lay on the purple comforter with night breezes fanning his soul, images of Muffy converged on the magical island he'd drawn in the bar.

With her, he could create fine art. With Chris and Mike, he could afford her. But with Chris and Mike, he'd spend all his time, all his energy, making nothing more than another video game.

Chapter Seventeen

The next morning, Muffy sat at her father's desk. She'd picked up the papers she'd whisked to the floor the night before and stacked them in neat piles. The certificates for the Everest and Richfield Funds, as well as her father's checkbook and latest bank statements, were ready for his accountant.

Dr. Sergeant's will and her trust papers were ready for their lawyer.

Until she'd sorted the contents of the safe-deposit box, she hadn't known her father had remortgaged the house. Like car insurance rates climb after accidents, malpractice insurance rates climb after claims are settled.

Muffy set the mortgage, house insurance policy, and utility bills in another pile. Next to it, she laid Dr. Pfeiffer's credentials and the income tax records from her father's practice.

Behind all the papers that had defined her life, she'd set a list of questions. Not the real questions, like where will I live? Should I find a better job? Does Peter love me? Merely the simple questions, like how much is my father's practice worth? Who has the authority to hire Dr. Pfeiffer? Who can fire Halliday and Crawford as trustees?

She had agreed to meet Peter at The Arts Center entry at 3:00. He had a surprise. As she waited for the men who would,

Sublime Recline 147

hopefully, set her financial life in order, she began seriously considering her emotional life.

She tried to picture moving in with Peter on the third floor. That would take care of a place to live. She had a car and, between them, they would find something to eat.

The problem is, I couldn't live with him in front of The Arts Center and the whole community.

As Grace greeted the men she expected, Muffy pictured Evelyn Richardson's disgusted sneer and the gossip wafting up from the pottery guild's new home.

I'll have to marry him. We can starve for a few years. He can test his talent and I can tell whether he loves me, my trust fund, or my model's body.

Go ahead. Take everything. There is a very fine, very gorgeous artist who wanted to ask my father for my hand. And if he didn't want to marry me, he never would have mentioned it.

Muffy floated through the rest of the day with a secret smile tucked in her mind.

She barely heard her lawyer agree to replace Halliday as her trustee. She forgot which one of them would negotiate the sale of her father's practice with Dr. Pfeiffer. There was also something about transferring money to her account and giving her authority to act as a clerk to pay her father's bills.

She didn't care.

When Grace turned on her cranky self, Muffy said, "It's an opportunity. Life with us has been so boring for you. Someone at The Arts Center needs you. I'll find out who."

At the emergency board meeting, she let Martin Sinclair take over. Poor Muffy, still grieving her father's death.

"Just vote yes."

She did. Halliday: out. Legal drafts: approved. Nominating committee: appointed. Next meeting: two weeks. Adjourned.

When she left the boardroom, Peter was nowhere in sight. Probably painting. She drove home and drew herself a cool bath with boutique salts. Would she have enough for five years of baths in the Haviland's deep old tub? No.

"It doesn't matter."

She couldn't wait to tell Peter he was right. There was a delicious freedom in losing everything. She felt lighter than she had in her whole life.

When she returned to The Center, Peter was waiting on the steps. "Hey," said Muffy. "Need a ride?"

"As a matter of fact, I do."

"Actually, why don't you drive?" She stepped from the driver's side door. Above her khaki shorts and caramel polo shirt, her golden hair shimmered in the sunlight.

"I'm almost a free woman." She beamed. "I've lost my family and my money, my home is on the market, and, who knows, my job could be next."

She slipped her arms around Peter's neck and gave him a passionate kiss. She felt both the warmth of comfort and the heat of passion. She savored both, imagining where they would lead once she was Mrs. Cinnsealaigh. What a sublime recline that would be.

She pulled away. With a husky whisper she said, "I have an idea. Since I scheduled my vacation for next week, why don't you join me at Streker's cottage."

"No," he said. "I mean, I've got that class."

"No problem. We'll come back for Wednesday morning. And I have another idea."

He kissed her smile. "Mine first."

Muffy slid into the passenger seat with the secret smile now blossoming all over her face. Peter wound through the country roads, raced along the Blue Route, and arrived in the heart of Bryn Mawr.

"You need some new clothes," he said.

"No I don't. I know mine are boring, but they're fine. More than fine. Made to last a long time."

He parked in front of a little shop. *Yours Truly* sprawled across the bright blue awning in white script. Mannequins in summer suits and straw hats posed in tall, thin windows on either side of the door.

Sublime Recline 149

"We're going shopping," he announced. "My treat. Buy anything you want, but nothing beige."

"I've never been here," she said.

He grinned. "I know. If you're as poor as you claim, you'll love it."

Muffy braced herself. Was it a thrift shop? A secondhand store? A place like Goodwill, where she sent Grace to donate her out-of-season clothes?

If I meet anyone I know, I can say I'm ... what? Selling my clothes to benefit The Center? Looking for costumes for a play? Yes. That will work.

Peter opened the door. Inside, the shop looked more like Renée Fortier's than Talbots. Clothes hung from recessed racks along the walls. Round tables, draped to the floor, held piles of cotton sweaters and leather bags. Everything looked new.

In the back, near a three-way mirror, two leather chairs waited at one end of an Oriental carpet. At the other end, a tiny woman with bright white hair was returning a tray of jewelry to a case beneath the register.

"Welcome," she said. "May I help you?"

"Size eight?" asked Peter.

Muffy nodded.

"Probably a dress, maybe a jacket, slacks. Anything but beige, white, gray, black, or navy."

The woman removed her glasses and gazed at Muffy. "Would you like to take this room and I'll bring things for you to try?"

Muffy looked at Peter. "If I'd known, I'd have worn heels."

"If you'd known, you wouldn't have come. Go. I'll wait here."

Muffy turned toward the fitting room. She knew how to do this, even if the venue and the companion were different.

The fitting room was generous. Pink light cast a soft glow on her skin, the tiny chair, and creamy carpet.

The white-haired woman knocked, opened the door, and hung a red dress and a soft violet jacket on the brass hook.

"I'll bring more," she said.

Muffy held the dress under her chin. It brought out the pink tint in her cheeks. She read the handwritten tag: $25. Just as pretty but way cheaper than Renée Fortier. Checking the label at the side of the zipper, she recognized an Italian name that hung in her own closet.

The new me. Or is it the old me? Different shop. Different colors. Different man waiting. Definitely a new me.

She removed her shirt and shorts and slipped the red dress over her head. As she struggled with the zipper, the white-haired woman returned with a quick knock. After hanging lavender slacks and an emerald green suit on the hook, she turned Muffy around and finished closing the dress.

Standing back, she said, "I believe it suits you. Do you want to show him?"

Muffy studied her reflection. The deep red brought out her color so well it almost looked as though she were blushing. She followed the woman from the fitting room. The leather chair looked as though it were custom-made for Peter, and he looked like he could sit comfortably for hours.

Muffy stood in front of the mirrors and turned.

"We'll take that one," he said. "Next."

She saw the dimples conquer his cheeks.

Returning to the fitting room, she tried the green suit. The sleeves were too long. She tried the lavender slacks and violet jacket. The slacks were too short. The jacket was perfect.

As she turned the knob, the woman opened the door. "Do you have anything else to go with this jacket?" Muffy asked.

"I would suggest, but your young man disagrees."

"Here," said Muffy, handing her the suit. "Could you bring a white skirt or slacks? Just to try?"

"Of course."

When she modeled the jacket with the long white skirt, Peter frowned. "I love the jacket," said Muffy. "I don't want the skirt. I just needed something to show you."

He rose.

Muffy checked her watch. "I'll hurry. I know you have to catch the light." *And I'm going to catch you.*

An hour later, she lay draped in the gauzy dress, draping herself over the dark velvet draped over the window seat. He'd altered the pose. Now she gazed at him and not the ceiling. Peter was gone; the focused artist stood in his place.

"I need the delight in your eyes while you tried on clothes," he coached.

She lay before him, exuding the joy she'd felt modeling the dress and jacket. She did have good taste. She could choose what suited her.

Muffy easily held her pose. The delighted expression on her face relaxed and then resurged as she sifted the details of her days with Peter from the rubble of the last month.

Peter noticed how the muscles of her legs and the planes of her face had softened. He had never seen her so peaceful. This evening he painted with a full palette. No hesitation. He knew exactly how much ultramarine and raw umber he needed to mix for the shadows of the drape.

He'd already captured the glint in her eyes. He had painted that first. It was the first thing he could remember wanting to keep.

He should have told her she could look away now, but he couldn't. She didn't speak, but her face revealed the joy in her mind more clearly than anything she could have said.

Beneath the nearly mechanical action of his eyes and hands, his mind teemed with poses, costumes, backgrounds. He could paint her for the rest of his life.

But to do that, he needed success. Income. A home.

The Mountain Dew waited, warming on the paint table he'd carried down from his room. A drink was a moment's diversion. It forced him to release his grip on the palette. Stretch his hand. Flavors released his mind from color and line just long enough to give him a fresh view when he returned. But with Muffy, he couldn't stop. He had to finish this weekend, photograph the painting, and send the slide to Philadelphia on Monday.

When he bent and squinted to check the shadow beneath her chin one last time, he realized he was out of light.

"Enough," he announced.

Muffy stretched one long leg and then the other, one long arm and then the other. But she didn't rise.

"Come here." She beckoned with one hand, holding the flute with the other.

Peter set the palette in its plastic box, looked for the jar of solution to clean his brushes, and realized he'd left it upstairs. Still holding his Filbert brush, he closed the space between them and sat by her side.

With glee in her eyes, she laid her free hand on the line of his jaw. She stroked the lobe of his ear.

With glee in her eyes, she laid her free hand on the line of his jaw. She stroked the lobe of his ear.

"When you asked my father for my hand," she whispered, "he didn't object. I think it would be fun to be The Arts Center residents together. Will you marry me?"

Before he could compose a softer arrangement, the words vaulted from his mouth.

"I can't."

Chapter Eighteen

Muffy's breath stopped. Her heart stopped. She stared at the babbling face before her.

". . . money . . ."

Muffy dropped her eyes to the hand still holding the flute. It was still attached to her arm. Incredible.

". . . contest . . . tell them . . ."

She found her toes. Nicely polished. Tasteful pink. Her own toes. Her body was sitting up, pulling the gauzy white skirt from under him.

". . . could I?"

Probably her feet were on the floor. They were below the rest of her. She looked back at the crushed velvet. She saw no scraps of herself scattered there. Neither a ripped heart nor an unhinged limb or an empty mouth littered the window seat.

"Did you hear what I said?" he asked.

"Sure." She looked through him and stretched her mouth, aiming for her practiced social mask. She knew she failed. Her lips were shaking and her face was burning.

As her bare feet skimmed the wooden steps, she felt like she was watching a video of herself. She felt the rush of air as Peter raced down the stairs behind her and surged ahead to block the door. His wide hands cupped her shoulders. Muffy froze.

"Alexandra," he said. "Hear me."

The steely shell Peter had softened over the past few weeks repaired itself in an instant. *Alexandra. Yes, Father.*

"Do you hear me?"

"Peter, I can accept—"

"I don't know if I can."

This Muffy heard. She held her breath, waiting for him to grin. Swing her around. Fix a date for their wedding in August.

"I would love to marry you," his serious self whispered, "but as I told your dad, the timing's not right. I drew cartoon characters and castles and lived like a pauper for seven years so I would have the freedom to be a real artist.

"Now who am I in love with? My muse. The woman I could paint for the rest of my life. The only woman who'd tempt me back to cartoons to support her."

"I see," said Alexandra. "We need to wait until you're a successful portrait painter."

He released her shoulders. In the twilight, shadows hollowed his cheeks and turned his eyes to forest green.

"Or," he said, "I can call Chris and Mike. They've got a new concept. A good one. It'll be game design twenty-four–seven for months, but we can squeeze in a wedding, buy a River Road estate, and live happily ever after."

Muffy felt the weight of the flute in her hand.

"I promised you a solo show, Mr. Gant. I have a show in the ballroom in August, but the smaller rooms are free. Your portraits are exquisite. Evelyn's apparently unimpressed with your still lifes, but currently, landscapes are selling. People want to view the natural world from the comfort of their homes."

She twisted the head joint from the body of the flute so that each hand was occupied.

"I'll be out next week. You'll be finishing your contest entry. We'll discuss your show a week from Wednesday. After your class. As for the marriage, you cannot abandon your calling and I cannot wait for another man."

Sublime Recline 155

She turned and forced herself to simply walk to her office. After closing the door, she settled the flute pieces into their velvet bed. For the third time that day, she pulled on her beige shirt and shorts.

After locking her office, she crossed a silent, empty entry and hung the gauzy costume on the banister. Stopped at the traffic light one block from home, a laugh erupted from her belly to her throat. By the time she parked under the portico, she was doubled over. Her sides hurt. Her eyes teared. She could hardly catch her breath. Had she ever laughed so hard?

The new, totally free Muffy sat in her car, engine running, cool air blowing, windows shut tight. The first sob melded with the last laugh. The little tears converged to trickle down her cheeks. She covered her face and slumped against the steering wheel.

Dusk closed the day. With her final sigh, she turned the ignition off. Silence. Peace. She pulled a tissue from the console and dried her fresh, new face.

Instead of bustling inside to sort papers, or touring the property of her past, she slid the seat back so she could stretch.

The fireflies stayed by the shrubs. Muffy remembered the summer after her mother died. She'd spent the weekdays at the Strekers. During those long, balmy evenings, she and Heather had scoured the hedges with their bug jars, competing to see who could catch the most fireflies.

Now, she couldn't even remember who'd won. All she wanted to do was return to that sanctuary.

The Strekers left the beach house at dawn on Monday morning. Whenever they raved about "that wonderful artist," Muffy applied her bland smile and switched the channel in her mind.

"Sure you'll be okay?" asked Mrs. Streker as she set a bag of new toys for Becca onto the backseat.

"I'll be fine," Muffy assured her.

"So nice you can be here. We hate to leave it empty. Call Al and Miriam if you need anything."

Muffy waved and the little banner of painted forget-me-nots

waved too. She gazed out at the water with no energy to swim. How could she have been so stupid? How could she have humiliated herself so badly? Was he sitting around The Center laughing at her?

No. He had looked so earnest. In fact, he had looked as sad as she felt. And he had let her make the decision. If it were that.

"Yes, Peter, my spoiled brat self demands that you throw away your dreams and marry me today. Right."

She sank into the sleek green Adirondack chair on the porch. Gulls squawked. Sparrows flitted around the privets. After her second cup of tea, Muffy closed the house and walked to the beach. The morning warmed while families staked their claims with coolers and chairs beneath bright umbrellas. Every time she saw a bronze-haired child, her heart stung.

Just forget him. Get on with your life. It's only been a month since James. You're just trying to fill the void that he and your father left. Slow down. You have plenty of time.

As she walked toward town, she repeated this mantra, hoping to believe it.

Few of the shops off the boardwalk were open. Muffy peered through the windows, hardly seeing the T-shirts and trinkets. Wandering down a side street, she saw an Asian man setting antique chairs on the sidewalk.

"Are you open?" she asked.

"Please," he said, gesturing toward the door. "Come in."

The shop was stuffed from floor to ceiling with books and bowls, rattles and rugs, lamps with beaded shades, and guitars with missing strings.

"Do you have any music?" she asked. "Sheet music or lesson books?"

"Ah, yes. Lesson book." His face lit up before he disappeared into the shadows at the back of the shop. When he returned, he carried a shallow box full of old lesson books with tattered red covers. Leafing through, he said, "Sorry. Only beginner."

"How much?" asked Muffy.

"Five dollar."

"For one?"

He shook his head. "Whole box. Good bargain."

"Two-fifty."

"Three."

Muffy pulled the little beige leather change purse from her pocket.

Back at the Strekers's, she opened the first book and held the flute to her lips. Holding her breath, she stared at the notes. They were meaningless symbols. They might as well have been Chinese characters.

You idiot. You can't read music. You must have played that little song by ear.

A new layer of stupidity covered the fresh collection. She pulled the flute apart and pushed the pieces into their places.

Between Mother and Peter, this flute has too many memories anyway. I should never have brought it.

She shut the case and opened her laptop. As the sun climbed into the afternoon and settled into the evening, Muffy lost herself in the numbers on the screen. Analyzing each Arts Center expense, she created a list of cuts. Analyzing each source of revenue, she created a list of enhancements.

Hunger finally grew from a subtle presence to a major distraction. As she opened the refrigerator, she could hear Peter's voice offering each dish. "How about a London broil sandwich? Look, we can add. . . . How about cheese? Remember, we had. . . ."

"Shut up, Peter. You're out of my life. Get out of my mind."

She finally chose crab salad and ate it right out of the plastic container as she stood by the window.

Watching the gulls glide so effortlessly, she thought of her father working so hard. And how hard Heather and Becca would fight the leukemia. And how hard Peter would have to work to succeed.

But is it even work for him? He loves it so much . . . I can see it in his eyes. He's even said it. It's all he wants or needs. Except for me. But that was just to model.

She returned the container to the kitchen and, defying a lifetime of parental warnings, changed into her swimsuit. On the beach, she left her cover-up by a small pile of oyster shells Becca had collected.

Each wave wet the next dry section of her suit. "Don't you ever swim alone, Alexandra," warned the old record of her father's voice.

It doesn't matter, Father, I've absolutely nothing to lose now.

She planted her feet and allowed the next wave to crest at her chin. Pushing off, she swam out far over her head to escape the memories of Peter's grin and dripping bronze hair. A touch of seaweed against her skin reminded her of tangling her legs with his during that slippery float to shore.

She floated on her back. A brilliant sunset filled the sky. Gold edged the low, pink clouds. Scarlet jet trails streaked toward the sun. Behind the luminous clouds lay a placid, pale blue sky. Muffy pointed her toes and fingertips, opening her heart to the beauty above her.

Her limbs remembered their winter ballet. Sweeping arcs in the water, she traced angels on the canvas of the sea. At that moment, the world was perfect. The water jostled her body with its invisible currents. Gulls called and waves crashed, each in its own perfect rhythm.

This is the reason for art. Great art captures the feeling I have now . . . but each of us longs to record it. We tell stories. We take photographs. Even the most inept of us try.

She thought about The Center. The exhibits. The fundraisers. The theater and classes. It wasn't enough.

Our real purpose is to share all we know with everyone we can reach so they can truly express what their souls can feel.

After a sprint to shore, Muffy wrapped herself in giant towels and opened her laptop. Ideas rushed from her mind through her fingers. Was this an ethereal gift from her father? Had the ocean washed the debris from her heart? Had that dazzling sky energized her mind?

A true smile relaxed her face as she typed the new mission statement for The Arts Center. A quiet voice whispered through the rush of projects filling her mind. *Losing so much has made room for you, Alexandra. Now to your own self, you too may be true.*

Chapter Nineteen

Peter's day was as busy as Muffy's was quiet. The photography teacher lent him a camera to take slides of Miss Sublime. Niki drove him to The Camera Shop in Philly, the only one he could find to process and return his slides in the same day. While he waited, he treated her to a sandwich at D-Whiz, a neighborhood deli.

"How's your boss?" He had practiced this question so much he had the carefree inflection almost right.

Niki laughed. Peter cringed.

"She'll probably be back tomorrow. She's a workaholic. Give her a day with nothing to do and she'll have parties and fund-raisers planned for the rest of the year."

So they haven't talked.

While they waited for Niki's BLT and Peter's pizza with the works, he filled three napkins with pencil sketches of his companion. There was a sleekness to her face—raw straight lines. Too easy to caricature, a challenge to soften.

"So now that you've got Muffy done, what are you going to paint?"

"Landscapes." He'd painted enough landscapes to last a lifetime. He had already profited from the public's love of losing themselves in places. How could he paint a farm or a forest and make it art and not illustration?

A fine artist can do that, Gant. Can you?

"Peter?"

"Sorry. What?"

"After you win the contest, everyone will want you in their galleries."

"I haven't won yet," he said.

"You will. How can you not?"

The waitress set a sandwich too large to bite before Niki. Peter moved the napkin holder and condiments to the side so his large pizza would fit on the table.

He chewed on the idea as well as the sausage, mushrooms, peppers, onions, olives, anchovies, pepperoni, and cheese.

"I've got to find a unique angle on the landscape idea," he said. "The Wyeths and their students have pretty much covered Chester County. Actually, the whole Brandywine Valley."

After dropping the envelope with the best slide, his business card, his bio and philosophy statement, his entry fee check, and, finally, his self-addressed, stamped envelope into the mailbox, he should have felt relieved. Before, he would have taken a break. Gone for a bike ride. Now his bike lay as twisted metal in a landfill.

"One more favor," he said. "You know where the Saab dealer is in Wilmington?"

The Saab looked new. The practical white box was built for safety first and comfort a very close second.

Peter had called Glen Rossiter that morning. His financial advisor had said, "Go ahead. You live rent-free. You'll only use it for business, right? It's a tax deduction."

Peter still hesitated. "You ever hear of Halliday and Crawford?"

"Bad news."

"What if I had a trust fund?" said Peter. "No access till I was thirty-five and I lost everything else. Could I claim hardship and draw from it?"

"Depends on how it was written. You setting up a trust?"

"No. Just a hypothetical question. So I could buy a car without—"

"Losing anything? Yes. Do it. A guy with the zip codes you've had this year, with no income or expenses, is going to flag an audit."

So he had spent the afternoon at the dealership buying the used car. He spent the evening sitting on the carpet in the art section of the library. Books reviewing the history of landscape painting lay open at his feet.

As he searched for inspiration in palettes and compositions, all he saw were Muffy's serious eyes.

How could I have let her go? Can't afford her. And she doesn't really love me. Her proposal was just a rebound from her father's death. Spoiled princess. If she can't have what she wants immediately, she doesn't want it.

Although this seemed true on the surface, his heart didn't believe it. She'd waited for James Waite. He couldn't ask her to wait for him.

He closed the book of Impressionist landscapes and opened his sketch pad. His left hand drew a path curving into a meadow. His critical mind sneered. *Path for pedestrians.*

He flipped the page and drew an oval pool. Willows and rain wept onto its surface. The critic was silent. Peter flipped the page. His hand recalled the lines of crashing waves and laid a thin outline on the page. Low horizon. Stormy sky.

Natural world. The natural world can be a wild and dangerous place you'd only want to see on a wall.

He flipped the page and drew a winter moon casting treeline shadows on drifted snow. Lost in memories of beautiful vistas, he nearly filled the pad.

"Sir, I'm sorry, but we're closing."

Silver toenails peeked from gold leather sandals just beyond his stack of books. He looked up.

"Would you like to check these out?" she asked.

"Sorry," he mumbled. "I'll put them back."

Back at The Arts Center, he parked the Saab in Muffy's slot. Niki had insisted. "Till we get your Resident's sign."

Sublime Recline

He turned on every light in his room and set a large pad of tracing paper on the easel. There, he spent the night refining his ideas with a charcoal stick and suggesting colors with scribbles of pastels.

At dawn, his bed and the floor were filled with preliminary sketches for his show. Storms to watch from a dry sofa. Winter nights to explore from a warm, sunny den.

None even hinted at human, animal, or cartoon character life. Neither castles nor caves, barns nor burrows intruded in the land of Gant. His world was not a sunny place. The lines were sharp, the colors dark.

He noticed. "Well, Peter the Gant, art comes from the artist and that's where you are. It's not Wyeth. It's not Winslow Homer. It's pure you."

He moved the drawings from the bed to the floor and sprawled across the purple comforter. Totally spent, his pose was far from sublime.

The next evening he sat on the front steps with Thea.

"So what are you doing for Fourth of July?" she asked. "Want to go to the shore?"

"No."

"Whoa. You're a little cranky."

"Sorry. I've got work."

"You need a break. What about the Poconos?" she suggested.

Peter imagined the boring July green of the mountains and shook his head.

"Fireworks in Philly?"

"She said natural landscapes."

Thea rose and strolled to her van. When she returned, she carried cantaloupe halves filled with fruits. "Here, eat this," she said. "Old Chinese recipe. It'll make you feel better."

"I have a couple friends," he said. "You make a picnic. I'll get drinks. They'll know where to go."

* * *

Peter painted quickly. Even though ten years of sketches now drifted as smoke far over the Atlantic, his hand held the memory of those lines. His mind turned the barrel on the kaleidoscope, rearranging those images again and again.

Registrations for the next summer session grew. The waiting list equaled the class.

"Would you teach two classes?" asked Niki. "One morning and one afternoon?"

"One morning, one evening. I need the afternoon light," he answered.

In his class, Peter was his uncensored self. "That's not the way it looks, Mrs. Hyatt. Put your brush down. Now look. Measure. Pretend the eye is a unit, like an inch. How many eyes high is the face? The nose long? Take that eye and measure the whole face.

"Here." He gave her the little pad and pencil he carried. "Go around the room. Sketch everyone. Don't worry about the details. Think eye units."

"Should I do that too?" asked Linda Briggs.

Peter glanced at her canvas. "No. You've got the proportions. You don't see color."

And so it went. He filled the whole three hours with short, individual lessons and blunt critiques. When he heard the grandfather clock chime 12:00, he vanished upstairs.

By July Fourth, he had several paintings nearly completed. He had wanted to have a show's worth finished, welcome Muffy back, and say, "Look. See my fine work. All done. Let's marry." Just like the video-game hero, he could present the princess with the gold and float out to the waiting carriage.

Instead, he met Chris, Mike, and Thea in the parking lot at Longwood Gardens. Thea charmed his friends with spicy satay, another spring roll experiment, and tales of Chinese ancestors.

Watching Chris, he wondered if his friend saw Thea, or a human version of Lara Croft. They finished their parking-lot feast with blazing red cinnamon ice cream before entering the gardens for the display.

"So where's your muse?" asked Mike.

"At the shore. You got a name for the game?"

"Not my job," said Mike, as he turned to Chris with a comment.

Peter trudged along the wide path, blind to the silhouettes of the giant beech trees against the dim sky and deaf to his friends' conversation. He wasn't sure whether it was the addition of Thea, or his mind still working out wilderness details. The chemistry just wasn't there.

Even when the fountains shot jets of water through colored floodlights under brilliant explosions all perfectly timed to the music he loved, he'd rather have been painting. More precisely, painting Muffy.

Muffy walked with the salty, sun-screened tourists from the boardwalk to Rehoboth Avenue. Strolling through the souvenir and craft shops, all she could think of was The Center.

Who would teach stained glass? Could we blow glass? No. What about a wood shop? Wood block prints. Finger prints. Finger painting. Children's camp. After school program. . . .

Her mind wouldn't stop. She marched to the boardwalk, sat on a bench with strangers, and opened her planner. When she had emptied her head of this batch of ideas, she rose and looked at the ocean.

Instead of seeing the gulls and umbrellas, she saw artists recording waves and clouds, shells and sand, grasses and waders in everything from inks to oils.

Writing it down didn't help. She wanted to talk. Share her excitement. Spin the ideas out of her head. She'd called Niki twice. Too busy.

She couldn't wait to tell the planning committee, but she knew she'd overwhelm them.

She really wanted to call Peter. He would share her delight and expand her ideas. All she had to do was push the button on her phone and say, "Peter."

But she couldn't. She had humiliated herself so badly that she dreaded seeing him tomorrow. She tucked the planner back in her bag and rose. Stopping at the saltwater taffy store, she picked up two boxes. She felt Dr. Sergeant lift an eyebrow.

She told herself that it was for Niki and Grace and then bought a third for herself.

A little girl with red-gold curls and a cone of blue cotton candy stopped before her. "Hi," she said. "Want a bite?"

"I'll trade you," said Muffy. She took a green taffy from her box and slipped it into the little girl's pocket.

The tiny tourist pulled a blue wisp from the whirl and held it up. As it reached Muffy's fingers, the girl grinned up at her mother.

The sugar melted as soon as it touched Muffy's tongue. She watched the little elf toddle down the boardwalk, sharing her treat with random strangers.

How would you capture this, Peter Gant? Would you see a generous angel? Or would you see me as alone as I feel?

Behind her, explosions thundered and sparkled in the sky.

Chapter Twenty

As the sun slid above the horizon, Muffy took her final dawn swim. Past the breaking waves, she lay on her back basking in that snow-angel frame of mind.

With all the ideas she had for the board, it would be a long time before she returned to Rehoboth Beach. She mentally thanked the Strekers again for this wonderful retreat.

Her heart still stung when she thought of Peter Gant. Especially when she reviewed The Center's rooms, reallocating spaces to make room for more classes. He could stay until fall. By then she would know what space she needed, what his plans were, and, most important, where she stood financially.

Thoughts of money were always connected with her father. And when he came to mind, grief, anger, compassion, and curiosity took turns coloring her memories. So much to sort through, but no rush to do it. Unlike the plans for The Center.

In her briefcase, she had brochures for the elegant, Victorian, beachfront hotel. It was a wonderful venue with off-season autumn rates for water lovers to record the essence of their joy. Arts Center sponsored. The first of many.

On her laptop, she had the grant request to fund an outreach program to the Shelter for Abused Women. Art could express pain as well as joy. Art could be a constructive, or at least a helpful release for sadness and rage.

Muffy rolled to her side and swam to just the right spot. Flipping onto her stomach, she rode the wave to shore.

Three hours later, she parked at The Arts Center. She wore her regular beige and a deep tan outside and a curdled mix of anticipation and dread inside.

The first change she noticed was the Resident sign before the slot next her own. The car filling the reserved place was a bright, white Saab.

So you can afford a pricey car but not a wife? You don't want a thing. Right, Mr. Gant. And where'd you get the money for that?

Muffy, stop. He cannot live out here without a car. He might have piles of money and just not want to spend it. On you.

She turned her back on the car and hurried up the familiar steps.

"Hey," said Niki. "You look great."

"Yeah? Well, it's good to be back. Is my desk buried?"

"Nothing urgent. Your only appointment is with the Resident at one." Niki waited, eyebrows raised.

"So he bought a car."

"He can't live out here without one. Wait till you see what he's done for his show." She started to describe dark landscapes and Muffy held up her hand. "Let him surprise me. Did you get my e-mail about having his reception the day after the Figure Society's? If he wins, it will be a perfect tie-in. If not, no harm done."

Muffy passed the morning answering calls and mail. For lunch she shared a sandwich and her favorite new ideas with Niki. To pass the rest of the lunch hour, she strolled out to the pottery guild's cottage. The door and windows were wide open. She heard his merry voice.

A contradictory mix of excitement and embarrassment, warmth and chill filled her mind and heart. Before she could move, Heather emerged from the door.

Sublime Recline 169

"Muffy, you look great. I'm so glad you could use the house."

"Me too. Thanks. How's Becca?"

"We get test results this afternoon."

Heather caught the floppy, flowered beach hat and set it back on the thin gold wisps at her shoulder. The child's dark eyes found the tall man behind her.

Peter appeared in the doorway, clean sheets and shirts hung over his shoulder. "Hi," he said to Muffy.

Becca leaned toward him with outstretched arms. He lifted her high, then pretended to drop her. She shrieked with delight. "Do you like to paint?" he asked.

She nodded and snatched the hat from her head once again.

"You have a beautiful head," he told her. "Shall I paint a flower on it?"

She smiled.

To Heather, he said, "We'll make it fun."

"Excuse me," said Muffy as she passed them and entered the cottage. The inside smelled of earth. Sunlight glazed a mask in the making. Women's conversations drifted with the dust motes in the air.

"How's your new space?" she asked.

Smiles and nods answered her.

Muffy mentally rearranged the benches and added a low table for children along the far wall. The laundry closet doors were folded open.

Is that necessary? Yes. Whether it's the artist or me, the Resident will need to do laundry.

How am I going to get over him if I have to see him here every day?

When she strolled back outside, Peter, Heather, and Becca were gone. She tried to enjoy the breeze on her cheeks and its motion across the grass. All she could see were his playful green eyes and how he'd delighted the sick little girl.

Opening the door to her office, she found him waiting in the side chair. He rose. "Have a nice vacation?" he asked.

"I did. I hear you've started your show paintings."

"Do you want to see them?"

In your room? Definitely not. Can I ask you to haul them all down? No.

"How many do you have?"

"Six. They're not finished. But it will give you an idea."

For no good reason, she checked her watch. Time had nothing to do with her actions. "All right."

She led the way through the door and stopped at Niki's office. "I'll be upstairs for a minute."

"Peter, here's your mail," said Niki with a huge smile.

He took it and shoved it in his back pocket.

Silence followed them up the stairs. Muffy climbed faster. All that remained of the sublime moments on the window-seat landing were the cushions. She stepped aside and let him lead. A mistake. Now she was forced to watch his tall, lean body and his graceful motions.

The door to his room was open. The breeze waving the grass was sweeping the heat out the windows. She smelled paint. The scent was even stronger as she entered the crowded room. On the easel and against every wall were drying canvases.

For some reason, she had thought small. Little paintings of the meadow out back, maybe a tree, a sunset. The works in progress were big. Powerful. Like the man himself. The scenes were lonely, brooding. She couldn't say bleak. The lines carried too much energy. He'd expressed, in totally different places, the feeling of abandonment and isolation she'd felt after swallowing the cotton candy.

"What do you think?" he asked. "Pedestrian?"

She shook her head and met his eyes. "No." She wanted to rave about each one. Tell him he was the most brilliant artist she'd ever seen. Tell him Evelyn would have to find witty positives to use.

"The Figure Society's reception is on the fourth, right?" she asked.

Peter shrugged.

"It's on the fourth. We'll hang that afternoon. If you win, it will tie in perfectly. If not, at least you'll have this. You finished the painting, right?"

He nodded.

"May I see it?"

"Not yet. It's not quite ready for viewing. If this is okay, I mean what you had in mind for natural, I need to get back to work."

Muffy took a deep breath. "These are fine. Bigger than I'd planned. I'm not sure where we'll put them, but we'll show them well."

Before she said some stupid thing to humiliate herself again, she left.

Peter slumped on the bed and felt the envelopes crush beneath him. Standing, he removed his self-addressed, stamped envelope from his pocket. Feeling the slide inside, he slid it behind the creamy square envelope addressed in calligraphy.

He opened the invitation first. The inside envelope read *Mr. Peter Cinnsealaigh and Guest.* He opened this envelope. The wedding would join Leah and James on July 29th at 4:00. The reception would follow.

Was Muffy's addressed to Ms. Alexandra Sergeant and Guest? Of course. Had she received it? Read it? Decided to bring someone else? Of course.

He dropped the invitation on the purple comforter and ripped the flap on the contest envelope. Congratulations, announced the form letter. Bring your work to the Philadelphia Convention Center, Saturday, July 29th between 12:00 and 6:00 P.M.

He thought he'd be ecstatic, but all he could do was sink to his bed. It could have been a beautiful day, riding to Philly in the nearly new Saab with Muffy the muse at his side. First, he'd deliver the Sublime Recline and then they'd return to the country chapel to dream of their own wedding while watching their friends'.

Instead, he would ride into Philly with Thea. Then he'd sit across the aisle and the huge gulf separating James Waite's friend from Leah's.

After eating Grace's chicken-salad supper, Muffy strode into her father's den. She tossed the junk mail into the trash unopened and stacked the bills in a neat pile. "I'll pay them later."

She held the invitation envelope for a long, sad moment before slitting the top. The inside envelope read *Ms. Alexandra Sergeant and Guest.*

She opened that envelope and read of James and Leah's request for her presence at their wedding and reception.

I want to come to your wedding about as much as you probably wanted to come to my father's funeral. Friends demand the most painful things from each other.

Muffy slouched in the high leather swivel chair wondering who she could ask to join her. Peter would have been fun. She tried not to imagine him at her side in some outrageous costume sketching the guests.

Since he's Leah's friend, he'll probably be there. With whom? His friend Thea? Some new model?

Muffy sat in the dim room and swiveled to face the light box where her father had studied so many X-rays. The gray screen blurred and images of Peter filled her mind.

You are a clever man, Mr. Gant. Would I have posed for you as a mere friend? Was it necessary for you to make me fall in love with you first?

Yes, sadly enough. And now you won't even let me see it.

The ringing phone delivered her from her dismal thoughts. "Miss Sergeant?"

"Dr. Pfeiffer, you can call me Muffy." She pictured him sitting in this very chair with books replacing the instrument collection and little children somersaulting across the carpet.

"The house is for sale too?"

"Yes. I think you should buy it. With the office in back, you would have more time for your family. Most doctors have

Sublime Recline 173

so little time for the ones.... Ones who would love them," she added softly.

He laughed. "I don't have a family. Not even a prospect. Once I'm established...."

"No? Hmm. Well, not to be forward, but I have an opportunity for you to meet some people in the community, introduce yourself as the new doctor in town. Are you free on Saturday the twenty-ninth?"

When she arrived for the following Monday's board meeting, The Arts Center's door was locked.

Of course. Probably out partying. Probably doesn't even sleep here anymore.

Opening the dining/boardroom, she imagined his solemn paintings on the walls. *They are too big for here. I'll have to rearrange things and use the ballroom. At least they won't be up for long.*

"Welcome back," said Martin Sinclair.

One by two the room filled with familiar faces.

"This will be very short," said Muffy. "Attached to your agenda is a list of high-yield bonds I suggest for half of the endowment fund. That will give us some operating funds.

"The funds that Henry Halliday chose are fundamentally sound, it's just that his timing was off and he put all the money in one basket. If we leave half the money there, we'll cover our losses when the stock market turns around.

"Also, I will take a salary cut of fifty percent for six months.

"Your third page is a new mission statement and a list of ideas. We can grow this center. We have the room, we just aren't using it. I'm presenting this to the program committee on Thursday. Read it over. If you have ideas to add, call me."

She heard nominations to fill the empty board seats. She heard Sinclair's smug report of visiting Halliday's office with a state trooper and a subpoena for The Arts Center records. And she heard the motion approved to appoint her acting treasurer until they could find Halliday's successor.

After the meeting adjourned, the parting conversation turned to Peter. "Does he have everything he needs?"

Muffy blew a long breath through pursed lips. The image of the merry man who claimed he needed nothing filled her mind. "I'm sure," she answered.

"Nice young man. Resident Artist, brilliant idea. Can you get him to do a children's class?"

"No." She hated the longing she felt seeing him with a child in his arms. "We pay him nothing. We cannot ask him to give more."

"Did he enter the Figure Society's contest?" asked Evelyn Richardson. "I'm judging."

Chapter Twenty-one

Peter couldn't park the Saab in front of the Convention Center. No space. He stopped in front of the door, removed the paper-covered canvas from the back, and instructed Thea to keep driving around the block until he came out. Carrying the painting of Muffy inside, he didn't look back.

He rode the escalator to the second floor and paced down the wide hall to Room 202A. Carpet, curtains, and clusters of soft furniture absorbed the sounds of the few conversations.

An anorexic woman with short, spiky red hair and huge, red-framed glasses sat at a long folding table staring at him.

"Name?" she asked.

"Gant."

"Peter Gant?"

He nodded.

"One moment."

She rose from her chair and hurried into the room beyond the curtained partitions. Peter's fingers twitched, eager to record the flutters of her gauzy skirt. Waiting, he turned and searched the room for his competitors' work. Nothing. It was probably stored in that back room.

"Ah, Peter Cinnsealaigh."

Peter turned and faced an impeccable, bespectacled wizard whom the red woman had conjured from behind the curtain.

"Let's see this beauty," he said.

Peter propped the canvas on the table and ripped off the brown paper covering.

The wizard studied the painting.

Peter held his breath.

"Well, Cinnsealaigh, I've been waiting nearly a decade for you to get ripe." He looked beyond Peter toward the hall. Then he scanned the chairs. "Where is she?"

"Who?" asked Peter.

"The nymph. You left her in the car?"

Peter shook his head. "No. Um . . . she . . . she's busy today."

The wise, critical eyes twinkled. "You'd better bring her along on Friday."

Peter had recognized the man from the first glance. Northrop Kingston. His nemesis and mentor. The force that drove him through his junior and senior years at PAFA. All that harping now reverberated in his head. "Watch those edges Cinnsealaigh. Measure. Is a mouth an eye high? Nothing you paint will be ultramarine blue or sap green. Look. Study. Mix your colors."

Kingston chuckled. "Now, she's just your muse? Got an agent?"

Peter exhaled all the breaths he'd held. "She could be everything. Little misunderstanding. Confused priorities."

"Yours or hers?"

Peter opened his mouth and closed it. He'd learned not to answer Kingston's trick questions years ago. He looked at the man now and waited.

"What else have you done?"

"Video games," he mumbled.

Kingston nodded. "Good money. Good profession for some. Not for you." His gaze strayed to Muffy and remained for an endless moment before he rediscovered Peter.

"What else have you painted?" he asked.

"I have a small show of landscapes at The Arts Center out

in Chester County. Opens tomorrow. And I've done a couple portraits."

"Arts Center. Hmm."

The old man's head bobbed. He paced back and forth in front of Muffy. He reached a forefinger toward the flute. Withdrew it. Pointed toward her bare foot. Brought his finger to his lip and tapped it.

Still studying the painting he said, "Some artists meet a muse, make one exquisite painting, and spend the rest of their lives trying to recapture that spark.

"Your top priority is to capture that muse. She brings out a gift I could never teach."

Peter tucked those words in the back of his mind. "Are you judging?" he asked.

"Not on your life." Kingston glanced at his watch. "Arts Center. Isn't Evelyn Richardson on that board?"

Peter nodded.

"She's the judge," said Kingston.

The last place Muffy wanted to be that afternoon was sitting at Mark Pfeiffer's side on a velvet-covered pew cushion in the tiny stone chapel.

Not that the late afternoon sun didn't ignite the reds and blues in the stained-glass windows. Not that the harpist didn't sound ethereal. Everything for James and Leah's wedding was perfect. It was even good to see their old friends whose hearts were big enough to welcome Leah without shutting Muffy out.

It was just that she was in love with the bronze-haired man across the aisle. She tried not to look, but failed. He sat with Thea two rows ahead. Muffy could stare at him for the whole wedding and no one would know.

She watched for those little hugs, quick kisses brushed onto an ear, and secret looks that new lovers exchange. She saw none. As she expected, she could see Peter's left hand recording his impressions in the little pad propped on his knee. If she were the one sitting ahead of him, would he be sketching her?

She had spent the last weeks trying to decide if she could ask Mark to rent her a room in her old home, cheap, for a few months. Until she resumed her full salary. She was sure he would, and sure he'd be a gentleman, and sure he would get attached.

She checked her watch. Four more hours.

I can tolerate anything for four hours. I think.

The harpist began the beautiful "Kanon" by Pachelbel. As Muffy stood, she saw James standing at the front of the church. With his black hair perfect and his deep blue eyes intent on Leah, he couldn't have appeared more handsome. But to Muffy, he was as exciting as a cereal box.

She turned to watch Leah and accidentally caught Peter's eye. Her breath caught and her heart raced. She tried to keep turning, but couldn't. He winked and kept staring right at her. His mouth widened and sent her a silent, "Hi."

Her face burned as Leah passed between them and broke the spell.

"Dearly Beloved, we are gathered here. . . ."

Outwardly, Muffy knelt and prayed, rose and sang, and watched Leah become Mrs. James Waite III. Inwardly, she wondered how Peter could be so blasé as to wink. Since she'd come back from Rehoboth, their paths had barely crossed. When they did, it was a brief greeting or a brief discussion about his show.

Peter saw Muffy glare at his wink.

Shouldn't have done that.

He shifted his gaze to lovely Leah and slipped the pad of sketches into his suit pocket. He tuned the minister out as well as the ruthless scolder in his head.

All the way from the convention center to the chapel, Kingston's words had played in his head. As always, the man's intuitions were right.

As much as he wanted to approach her at the reception, he couldn't let his blunt mouth sabotage him again. He would wait and plan until he knew exactly what to do.

* * *

All through that hot week, Muffy loved her work, sorted generations of Sergeant possessions, and successfully avoided Peter Gant. She also avoided the second-floor window seat. Then came Friday.

Late in the morning, she raced upstairs to check with the children's craft teacher. Verifying attendance, she hoped to place some of the wait-listed children.

After finding the class full and telling a dozen little artists their clay models of feet and hands were brilliant, she retraced her steps down the hall. Movement drew her eye over the seat and through the window to the meadow where Peter stood holding Becca.

Her little, bare head was covered with painted petals of red, yellow, and orange. Green points curved toward her cheeks and forehead. The pair of artists faced the easel, each left hand holding a brush. Becca dabbed green on the tiny canvas and then on Peter's cheek.

He turned in mock horror. Glee sparkled in Becca's eyes and widened her smile. Peter kissed her nose, set her down in the miniature Adirondack chair and handed her the canvas for her own art.

Muffy had seen him change from man to artist enough to know what was happening even from this distance. The brush was quickly wedged between his ear and hair. His sketching hand was already leaving lines on the pad on the easel.

As the adults from the morning classes passed her, she couldn't move. She looked at the window seat where she had played her heart's own song through the golden flute. Where she'd allowed him to capture her soul on canvas.

Tears blurred the image of the artist and his tiny subject. She wondered how her portrait had turned out. Niki had told her the painting was accepted. He'd brushed off her congratulations. Had he won? The reception was tonight. No matter where his heart lay, she had a right to see that painting. She tipped her head back and fluttered her eyelids to absorb the tears.

That afternoon, between questions and phone calls, she decided to appear at the Convention Center and see the painting for herself. After closing her office, she strolled through the ballroom, checking his landscape exhibit one more time. She wondered if Evelyn would see his talent or simply award the prize to a friend. Would she praise this exhibit or exercise her critical vocabulary? The worst of it was, Evelyn's eye was right. She could see success years before it bloomed. Collectors read her column to buy up early work.

Peter found her in the ballroom standing before *Sparse Season,* his winter woodland scene. Although he hadn't crept up on her, she hadn't seemed to hear him.

"Is that your favorite?" he asked.

"No." She turned to face him. "My favorite is *Sea Swallow.* I keep searching through your clouds and waves for the bird. But that's not what you meant, is it?"

He found himself by her side. "No," he answered.

"What did you name my portrait?" she asked.

Her eyes revealed the most vulnerable soul he'd seen since her proposal. He wanted to swallow her now in kisses.

Not yet.

"That's why I'm here," he said. "Would you come with me to the reception? You can see for yourself."

"Why wouldn't you let me see it?" she asked.

"Because I'd compare it with the real you and I'd want to fix it and if I started I wouldn't stop. And I had a show to paint. Can you leave now? Did you keep the red dress?"

Muffy nodded. He led her outside to the shiny, white Saab.

The interior belied the car's age. The carpet was clean, but worn. Stray threads dangled from the stitching of the beige leather seats.

"I have CDs in the glove box," he said. "Pick anything."

"The Old Castle" in "Pictures At An Exhibition" had barely begun when he reached the Sergeant house. "Take your time," he said, "I'll wait right here."

Muffy slid from the car and marched into the house. Disappointment hung in her heart as heavy as a dripping sponge. From the moment they'd met, he'd only wanted to paint her.

He'd been a friend. He had taught when she needed a teacher. At her father's funeral, he'd been there, by her side.

"My friend Peter," she mumbled as she lifted the dress from the far end of the clothes rod. "My friend James. My friend Mark Pfeiffer."

I lied to you Peter. I love all your work the best. I would buy it all and hang it wherever I wound up living.

She zipped her dress and brushed out her silky hair. After transferring a few essentials to a white purse, she trudged down the stairs.

"Grace?"

Silence. Muffy peeked in the housekeeper's room. Empty. Glancing out the kitchen window, she saw him posing her on the steps under the portico.

Always the artist. I didn't mind posing. I loved lying there watching you paint. But posing's not enough for me.

She watched him tilt Grace's chin. She saw the focus in his eyes. *If I leave him with her we'll miss the whole thing.*

Muffy bustled out the door. "I'm ready. Come on."

Peter rose. "I need a background. Let me think about that. You find a costume. Something—"

"Peter, you'll be late." Muffy smiled at Grace and rolled her eyes. "He's really got to leave now. I promise he'll be back to paint you."

Grace cocked her head and crossed her trim ankles. "I'll be here," she cooed.

The traffic going into Philadelphia was thick; the traffic coming out was practically parked. Peter aimed the car toward the city.

Muffy, owner of the recently bruised heart, sent pages of questions to her mouth. Alexandra, director of board meetings, ignored them and watched the paint-stained fingers holding the steering wheel and shifting gears. She studied the long legs pressing and releasing the pedals.

After leaving the car in the parking garage, Peter set a brisk pace to the Convention Center. Inside, she saw the sign:

Philadelphia Figure Society
Presents
Sublime Recline

He hurried her to the escalator. When it finally reached the top, a trim matron in summer black handed them programs. Peter took Muffy's before she could see it and led her through the door.

There, hung on a dark, curtained partition, was *Siren's Song,* the first-place winning painting. As the sun set behind her, an ethereal nymph serenaded her love with a golden flute. Golden hair framed her face as it had the first time he'd asked her to free it. Her eyes asked, and promised.

Muffy stood awestruck. His gift was greater than she'd even imagined. And she was this artist's model, his muse.

She felt someone staring and turned. A little man with a cap of gray frizz, black tux, and red bow tie was glancing between her hand and her hair.

"You are?" he asked.

"Alexandra Sergeant," answered Peter.

The wizard nodded and turned back to Muffy. "Fine name for the portrait painters, but I'm not sure it suits you." Northrop Kingston winked at Peter and then vanished into the crowd.

Evelyn Richardson appeared wearing a swishy black dress. She handed Peter a long envelope. "My comments, in case you don't get Sunday's *Inquirer*. Muffy said you painted all those landscapes in a month. Is that right?"

Peter laughed. "Yeah. I was taking my time. Should have done ten."

Evelyn laid her hand on his sleeve. "Seriously, you could earn a living painting. I've only said that to one other artist."

Dropping her hand, she turned to Muffy. "Nice find. You saw something I missed in his first show. I'm buying his *Sparse Season.*"

As Muffy recalled the stark winter scene, a too-thin man in

a very well-tailored suit jabbed Peter's shoulder. "So this is what you've been doing."

"Hey, man," said his partner, a chubby man with thick glasses and a rumpled white shirt. "Way cool game. *Siren's Song*. Music theme. Scylla and Charybdis. Lots of nymphs. . . ."

Muffy pictured the mythical women singing from the rocks to lure the ancient Greek sailors to their deaths. *Too bad I couldn't distract him from his painting. But I wasn't playing the flute. I was simply posing.*

"No," said Peter. "Chris, Mike, this is Alexandra Sergeant.

Another man offered his warm, firm hand. "Nice to meet you," he said. "Glen Rossiter." He took a card from his jacket pocket. "I've made money for Peter in this bear market. If you ever need a second financial opinion, just call me."

He slapped Peter on the shoulder. "Nice work, Cinnsealaigh, but you don't do her justice."

Muffy put the card in her purse. *Made money in a bear market? If he had enough money to invest, why couldn't he marry me?*

"Peter," said Mrs. Pearlman. "Oh, Muffy, it's you. That color suits you, dear."

"Hello, ma'am," said Peter from a two-dimpled smile. "You like?"

"Exquisite. Here," she said, handing him an envelope. "A check from the insurance company for the fire damage. But young man, do you have a marketing plan?"

"You received the invitation to tomorrow's reception, didn't you?" asked Muffy.

"Of course, dear. I'll be there. But I meant long-term."

"We need to work on that," said Peter. He took Muffy's hand and led her from the crowd of friends to a quiet corner of the exhibition room.

"Speaking of long term—"

"I don't understand," she said. "If you have enough money to hire a financial advisor—"

"When we sold AxshunArtz, I made a couple million. I didn't have a clue, but I figured at even one percent interest, I'd have enough to live on, if I lived carefully. Glen's always talking asset allocation and growth this and value that, but all I needed was enough for paint and canvases. That is, until I met you. And, I'm not blind. I see how you live. My one percent wouldn't pay a mortgage in your world."

"But—"

He laughed. "Now I know I can make it painting fine art. If that won't support us, I have a backup plan. And Glen says if the market ever—"

"So the timing's better now?" asked Muffy.

"Timing's perfect. We've added one bright dress to your wardrobe, Ms. Sergeant. Would you add one bright name to your own?"

"Only if it's Cinnsealaigh, Mr. Gant."